"Terribly good and horribly pertinent"

Stephen Fry

what if ROALD DAHL wrote all about 2021...
Copyright © 2021 Geoff Bunn, Sally Bennett

First Printing: 2021
ISBN: 9798466626896

what if ROALD DAHL wrote all about 2021...

A collection of

Dahl-like short stories

SET IN 2021

by

GEOFF BUNN

Contents

Introduction

Like many kids growing up in the 1970s and 1980s, I watched **Roald Dahl's "Tales of the Unexpected"** with a mixture of grisly fascination and shuddery disgust. Bizarre, sinister, macabre and amusing were the sort of words used to describe Dahl's wonderfully disturbing short stories, transformed into television dramas and shown, I think, lateish on a Saturday evening.

We all watched them and we all enjoyed them, even if, often, they gave us nightmares an hour or two later once safely tucked up in bed. And the next day, Sunday, they were invariably the TV programme everyone was talking about. (Unless, of course, Manchester United had lost heavily again on 'Match of the Day').

In fact, although 9 series were made, totalling 112 programmes in all, from as early as Series 2 other writers contributed stories and the title was changed from *'Roald Dahl's Tales of the Unexpected'* to *'Tales of the Unexpected – Introduced by Roald Dahl'*. And it's partially with that idea in mind, to contribute to the pool of Dahl-inspired literature, that I have written and produced this book.

Roald Dahl himself wrote at a time where the world was undergoing severe stresses and strains. A wartime fighter pilot and intelligence officer, he saw first hand the sorts of horror humans were capable of inflicting upon one another. The second world war, rationing, the cold war, the nuclear age, Vietnam, the 1970s oil crises Dahl's world was very much a place of upheaval, doom and destruction.

Of course, I can't easily imagine what Mr Dahl would have made of our own difficult times: things like Brexit, Donald Trump, the Black Lives Matter movement, Covid, Putin's Russia or any of the other innumerable things that shape, change, reform, plague, enhance or pester all our lives today... but I do hope that some of the stories in this book come close, at least in parts, to the kind of thing he might have had to say.

I'd also like to take this opportunity to say a big & special thankyou to Sally Bennett, for her contribution to this book. With luck, we will NOT need to write another one of these in 2022...

Safe

In another country, very far away but uncannily similar to our own, little Johnny ate paint.

He ate it not just now and then, but regularly.

All sorts of paint.

And, as you would expect, eating the stuff made him rather poorly. Especially when, on one occasion, he actually helped himself to a great big gloopy spoonful or two of thick gloss white paint. The really strong stuff. The sort of paint that makes your brush go hard in a matter of hours. *That* paint.

Why did he do that?

Who can say.

Maybe it had been the cute looking dog on the tin of paint which had tricked Johnny into thinking the nasty stuff was secretly a rather nice treat which horrid adults were cruelly keeping to themselves? Yes, that was certainly one possibility. Though, to be fair, the dog on the tin ought to have suggested dog food really, rather than some delicious secret human food.

Or, maybe, the thick white paint had all too easily become confused, in little Johnny's tender mind, with double cream – albeit double cream without strawberries and in a super-sized metal tub? After all, it did look a bit like cream. A *little* bit. Though, to be fair, even the teeniest, tiniest slightest taste of it ought to have quickly disabused him of this notion.

Or, as a third possibility, maybe it was simply the case that little Johnny was just not ideally suited to thrive in this modern world of ours? A part of the process of evolution. The proof of the saying "Survival of the fittest"? Those who consumed paint, to such a level that it made them ill, and especially those who did it often, were – it could be argued – not truly destined to achieve a long and satisfying life.

Of those three reasons, it was hard to say which was the exact cause. His parents, however, were naturally very keen to blame the picture of the cuddly dog on the tin. And so they wrote, several times, to their local MP to make sure that:

1. the dog was removed from the tin and

2. everybody else was made thoroughly aware, in triplicate, of the dangers of eating spoonfuls of gloss paint.

"But... but we've been using that dog for decades", said the Chief Executive Officer of the paint company, slowly, incredulously shaking her head. "And no one has ever eaten our paint before".

"Yes, sure", replied the head of PR for the same organisation. "You know that, I know that, everyone in the factory knows that. But I'm afraid the dog has to go".

"But... but surely, it must taste disgusting. I mean, it's paint. It's horrible. How can anyone eat it?"

The head of PR nodded in agreement, but the fact was that the dog had to go. And so, reluctantly, they agreed to discuss the matter at the next board meeting.

And, within 12 months, sure enough, the dog was gone. Replaced with a cartoon brick wall, covered in graffiti. The idea being to make it abundantly clear that this was a tin of paint and not, in any way shape or form, something cuddly, cute or edible.

More than that, however, from here on an incredibly thick sheaf of instructions was to be included, with every tin of paint. People were told, in 17 languages, how to open the pot of paint, how to use a brush, how to dispose of the paint tin once empty and, most importantly of all, how to avoid eating the stuff or, even, being tempted to eat the stuff. "It may look like a scrummy thick cream, ideal to be served with strawberries", read the leaflet, in French, Serbian, English and even Armenian, "But it must never be consumed as such. Not even on a hot day, not even with an extra helping of sugar to make it go down better".

Had that been the whole saga, that would have been of no great import. One advertising logo gone. So what? Who cares?

But paint, sadly, was only the very beginning. Because Johnny, small as he was, at the still-eating-rusks sort of age, had revelled in the extra attention his doting parents paid to him as a result of his guzzling the paint.

He had also revelled in the attention he had received from the media.

And he had also revelled in the attention from the paint company and many others.

His toy collection had grown, exponentially, with every new photo opportunity. As did the number of glowing comments. As did his ego. Small as it still was.

And so somewhere inside that child, because of the dog, or the paint, or the madness of the world, or all three of those things, was born the seed of a mission: unable yet to expound his ideas, Johnny was nevertheless was about to undertake a lifelong crusade to make everything safe.

Everything. Safe.

All of it.

A year or so later, at the tender age of four – the very day after his birthday, in fact, and this despite the claims of his parents that they loved him so very, very much and really,

really, really wanted to keep him at home just a little bit longer, but, sadly, could not manage it and, truth be told, he simply had to start school at the first possible opportunity because of the pressures of work, and Grandmother not being what she was and so on and so forth – little Johnny started at infant school.

'Whitemead Junior and Infant School' had been up and running, educating kids, and doing a thoroughly good job of it, since the early 1950s.

Hundreds, if not thousands, of children had fond memories of their time spent in its classrooms. Singing in choirs or making things out of wood, or playing in a sandpit, doing basic physics or elementary maths. Days off for toothache. Looking forward to summer holidays. Birthday parties, Christmas carols, story competitions. All sorts of things. Kind teachers with their hearts in the right places. Doing the best they could on an all-too-often limited budget.

Basically, the stuff of most junior and infant schools throughout the land.

Innocent and warm, a local school for local nippers.

Alas, all of that was to change, or to begin to change, from the day little Johnny arrived...

His paint-eating days now over, no sooner had he entered the classroom than Johnny's attention turned immediately to the pens and pencils being offered to him. In particular, his big eyes widened hugely at the sight of great big chunky and colourful wax crayons.

On the one hand, to Johnny, clearly all of these writing and drawing implements were things to eat.

But on the other hand, deep inside, at an almost subliminal level, Johnny also recognised these things for what they assuredly were: deadly dangerous.

And before he had even been in the room long enough to need a wee – it was his first day, after all and so a wee wasn't all that long in forthcoming – he was biting chunks off a red wax crayon and crunching away on a pencil as it if were a stick of liquorice.

Perhaps unsurprisingly, after only a mouthful of pencil, he began to choke.

Maybe that would not have happened without first consuming the great gobbets of wax. Who could say?

Either way, he was promptly introduced to the Heimlich manoeuvre and the offending pencil was rapidly disgorged.

Crisis over.

But then, as soon as the teacher turned her back, he started on the pen. A plastic biro. Which, to be fair, even Johnny quickly realised was properly inedible.

The jar of ink, however, which came with an old fashioned fountain pen, was not so obviously unpalatable. And he downed the entire bottle in a few large gulps.

The disgusting taste did not appeal.

And so he grabbed another wax crayon and ate that. Whole.

Needless to say this hasty, and rather early lunch, given to and consumed by a four-year-old child, on only its first morning in a classroom, did not bode well for the young and enthusiastic teacher.

As for Johnny himself, he made a full and fast recovery. In no time at all. A small cut or two to his gums from crunching on the biro and the pencil, and a very peculiar tint to his tongue which lasted a full week. That was it.

But his parents stubbornly refused to let the matter pass.

Firstly, as they made very clear to the head teacher, these items were dangerous things for an unguarded child to have in their possession.

Of course they were.

And so there was very little the teacher, or the Union, could say in defence of the teacher, when she was summarily dismissed for her careless disregard of the all-too-obvious dangers of crayons, pencils, pens and ink.

But the parents wanted more than that.

It was clear to them that no child should ever again, not *ever*, be left alone with such terrible things.

And to achieve that end, they wrote again to their MP.

One letter.

Two letters.

Three letters.

The third letter finally rattled the MP, as the implication was that he would somehow be to blame in the future if any more children drank ink and so forth.

In turn, the MP rattled the media, and the media rattled Whitemead School – as well as other local schools – and forced them all to take action.

From then on, pens (and pencils) would only be issued under strict supervision.

As part of all this, of course, and with more than one passing reference to his earlier media stardom, Johnny received – and very much enjoyed – a lot of extra attention.

More toys came his way.

More fuss.

And his ego grew ever larger.

And so did that inner mission. Though he was still too young to see it clearly, he certainly felt its presence growing within him.

Other things soon followed.

At school, exercise was quickly banned due to the risk of injury. As were the sandpits. Because they contained dirt. As were field trips, ghost stories and even carol singing concerts. For each and every event, a reason could be found – and was found – to show just how potentially dangerous and bordering on the positively lethal any given thing could be.

"We must make sure none of our children are exposed to the dangers of X or Y or Z". That was the opening sentence of the school governors' very next meeting.

Every head in the room nodded in agreement.

Though none of them could have explained why they had agreed. Not really, not if pushed. After all, hadn't the school functioned perfectly well for years and years without any major incident? The odd small burn or scraped knee, yes. But nothing more than that. Was there really a need to now fence everything off and put signs all over the place such as 'Caution! This hot water can get hot' in the little washrooms and other notices such as 'Caution! A wet floor may become slippery'?

Similarly, hadn't they all grown up in a world with those things? And hadn't they all managed to survive until adulthood? Clearly they had.

So no. Had they actually stopped to think about it, not one of them would have agreed.

But under the pressure of the meeting, under the scrutiny of the media, and with the likes of Johnny's parents in the background, the signs went up anyway.

Because now the pattern had been set.

From here on, children must be kept safe. Kept off things, kept away from stuff. Things must be signed for, checked in, checked out. The correct shoes must always be worn. Coats in the rain without exception. Mittens and scarves. Heating must be kept at a certain level. Everything that might have come into contact with the floor would be bleached. And then everything that was bleached would be labelled to say that it had been bleached. Everything that might have come into contact with an animal, mucus, sweat, any sort of chemical, the outside, the inside – horror of horrors – would all be BANNED. End of.

Every child must be safe.

Totally.

Always.

Even if that meant taking things to silly or beyond silly levels.

And so it was that, at school dinners, the pink blancmange was labelled as having pink colorants. And the pink colorants were labelled as being artificial. (As if the blancmange itself was not!)

Lettuce was washed. In chlorine. To make sure it was thoroughly clean. And then it was labelled as being washed in chlorine to make sure the chlorine intolerant avoided eating the stuff.

Anti-slip flooring had to be put on the stairs. And then signs had to be put up to draw everyone's attention to the fact that there was anti-slip flooring, and that it was here because these were stairs and stairs were obviously incredibly dangerous at the best of times...

And so it went on.

Everything.

Everywhere.

No part of the school was untouched. Nothing was left to chance. It all had to be made not only safe, but super safe.

And then?

And then attentions were turned to the world outside school...

Oh my.

A long time ago, someone, we have no idea who it was, said that "If a butterfly flaps its wings in the Amazon, it could ultimately cause a tropical storm in Florida". Or some such nonsense.

Of course that wasn't true. Like so many of those daft sayings, it was taken entirely out of context.

However... in the case of Child Safety, it really was true.

Starting with the dog on the paint tin, then the pens and pencils and the ink and crayons at one junior school, the malaise spread outwards. Ripples of insanity all radiating outwards from little Johnny.

And so it was that, within a few years, every single mile of the tens of thousands of miles of railway lines in the country, were 'totally protected' with a high, ugly and expensive steel fence. (Lord help you if, somehow, you got stuck on the inside. The fenced finally ended at Wick, in the far north of Scotland!)

Where once children had been allowed to meander across a railway line, perhaps to reach a little minnow-filled stream on the other side, now that was all out of bounds. Off limits. Forbidden. The stream drained, fish killed, fields turned into car parks for those awful 'parkway' developments and the public footpaths closed.

Safety would come first. In all things.

The same was true of high places. Every high place. Even places that were not actually all that high. Things like Blackpool Tower were understandable – had it existed in that other country because, remember, all of this was taking place somewhere else. Safety up there *did* make sense. But now even places no higher than two storeys, such as old bridges or the end of a pier, were suddenly, all of them, fenced off. Closed. Restricted. Signs put up.

And it spread further.

And further.

The safety madness.

The mania.

Not only children but everyone, everywhere, MUST be kept safe. That was the new motto. That was the driving force...

"Hello, is that 999?"

"Yes it is. Do you need an ambulance, police or fire brigade".

"Ambulance please".

"What's the issue?"

"My grandfather. He's had an accident..."

"In the house?" said the voice at the other end of the line with a distinctly resigned tone.

"Yes. How did you know?"

The emergency was an all too familiar one. An old person, who had grown up in that treacherous world of insecure railway lines, dogs on paint pots, sharp pencils, ink and dirty knees, had cut their hand open. And the cut was a pretty bad one.

How had they done that?

On a child-proof lid, of course. Because in the panic to secure everything, everywhere, even things like cans had become much harder to open. And many of these things were especially difficult for older people who had poor eyesight or not such a strong grip.

And so to open a child-proof product, they frequently resorted to using knives, sharp and genuinely dangerous, to force the lid on something. A jam jar, perhaps.

One slip. Yes. And it was time to call the ambulance.

Another incident?

Yes. A builder had just been run over. And this was no short-sighted or weak-wristed aged person. This was an adult male down.

How had this accident happened? Surely it couldn't possibly have had anything to do with Johnny and his subconsciously-begun crusade... could it?

Could it? Yes!

The builder had been working in the city centre on a building site, wearing a high-visibility vest, goggles, a safety mask and safety boots, and he had been doing all of that behind a wall of noise emanating from those reverse beepers, those endless pointless alarms that tell everyone a vehicle is reversing.

Then his mobile phone had rung.

He had ignored it.

Then it had rung again. And a third time. Vibrating.

"Oh flip", he said (or words to that effect), "I'd better answer it, I suppose, it might be someone important".

But the noise on the site made answering the phone impossible.

All he could hear – all anyone for three miles around could hear – was the racket of those reversing beepers.

So he took a few steps off the site, and tried to find a place where he could hear and be heard. But his mask had thoroughly steamed up his goggles, and his heavy hat, boots and thick protective gloves and clothes made his movements ponderous.

Amid the alarms and the signs, and the misted goggles and the endless ringing phone, the road and the pavement easily blurred into one.

And then a big red bus ran him over.

By this time, of course, Johnny was about to finish at school. Aged 16 or 18 or something like that. (There were plans to raise the school leaving age to 43. Just to be on the 'safe' side).

The world had changed a great deal since his first swallow of paint. And, it had to be said, that change was almost entirely for the worse. Where once people, and especially children, were allowed to do things – now they were not.

However, there were still some things out there which had not yet been secured. Not yet made safe.

And on his first day at college, the idea came to Johnny that he needed to do something about the windows on the sixth floor.

In fact all windows.

Yes.

All of them.

Windows, it seemed to him, were clearly very dangerous things.

How had humanity survived for so many years with windows that opened? Johnny had no idea.

And as he sat there, alone, in the classroom at break time, on the sixth floor of the building, he began to draft a letter of his own to the local MP, demanding that something be done about those obviously hazardous panes of glass from which a person could so easily tumble.

It didn't take him long to write the letter.

And, as he finished it, he read it out loud.

Feeling quite pleased with himself.

Then he read it again.

And felt even more pleased with himself.

All the time, unaware that someone was listening. Someone out there, standing out in the corridor.

"Yes", said Johnny to himself, checking his sandwich for any dangerous fillings before taking a large bite of it. "Now I see it clearly. I do not need to be here, in college. I am a true entrepreneur! I need to set off, out into the world, as soon as possible and make sure that everything is safe for children. And for adults too, I suppose. Everyone. Though my focus will be on children, for it is they who must be protected, to the nth degree, from all these ghastly, horrible hazards such as windows".

The early praise, the toys, the media interest, the indulgent parents, had all played their role.

Somehow, at some point, little Johnny had completely lost the plot.

His ego had outgrown his still young and inexperienced brain.

"I know what I shall do", he continued. "I shall form a political party, that's what I'll do. And I shall call it..."

At that moment a helicopter flew across the sky.

Johnny watched it for a moment. And then his huge ego saw it as a sign.

"Helicopter", he said. "Yes! Of course! I shall call it the Helicopter Party. Those machines are always there, overseeing things, hanging overhead, they never miss a trick".

His voice began to rise and to boom, in the classic dictator-having-a-rant style.

The person out in the corridor moved. Just a little.

Back in the room, feeling very proud of himself, Johnny continued. Now getting incredibly excited.

"We will take power from all those other... from all those other careless and – evidently – utterly ruthless political parties who have allowed so very many life-endangering things to go unchecked for so long".

He stood.

Strode around the room a little.

"Yes! And people will flock to me, to my party, because I am the one who will make our world safe".

He strode around the room a bit more.

Walked over to the window.

Stood beside it. And looked down on the people below.

His people. That was how he saw it.

He would save them all.

"It was I!" he bellowed, though no one far down below could hear a single word. "It was I who instigated all of this. This clean and safe world in which we now live. It is thanks to me, perhaps indirectly, but nevertheless it was down to me, that swings and see-saws no longer pose a danger to children. They can no longer go too fast or swing too high. It is down to me that the corner of every road has a steel barrier, funnelling you all towards the crossing and stopping you from crossing the road at random places. It was because of me that train windows can no longer be opened. It was me who put..."

He hesitated and looked around.

Where was it?

Ah yes. Up there. In the corner of the room above the door. Keeping an eye on the empty classroom.

"It was me, me alone, who put all these wonderful CCTV cameras in every room, every home and on every street corner. Making our towns and yes, our countryside too, safe. Where children once foolishly played, but encountered such terrible and awful remorseless danger such as dirt and tadpoles, now they sit, secure and safe, at home, face to face with virtual reality. For no one can come to any harm on a computer".

He stopped. Enormously puffed up with a ridiculous pride.

Yes. He could see it clearly now.

His parents would be proud. Wherever they were. (It had been some years since they told him they were taking a short holiday, leaving him in the care of his aunt, who quickly left him in the care of a sister, who quickly left him in the care of a guardian, who quickly...).

Johnny's future would be glorious.

Children would have nothing to fear. Not any more. Not anywhere. Not ever.

Sure to be elected on a huge popular landslide, the Helicopter Party would make the world a thoroughly sterile place!

Safe. That was the word.

He ranted. He railed. He crowed.

Suddenly the figure that had been lurking in the corridor burst into the room.

A girl.

A girl in tears.

"So it was you, you swine! You that got my Mom sacked from her job at Whitemead all those years ago!"

The girl ran straight at Johnny.

"You little shit!" she screamed. "You broke my Mom's heart! She loved being a teacher!"

Johnny stood stock still. Aghast. But that didn't prevent the girl from crashing straight into him. Furious as she rightly was.

Crashing into him, in fact, with such force, that Johnny was flung backwards. Clean off his feet.

Clean off his feet and straight through the wide open and evidently dangerous sixth floor window.

Oh dear.

Oh dear.

Oh dear.

And it was such a long, long way down.

And even the ugly netting far below – set up to prevent pigeons from staining the college pavements and thus (presumably) spreading noxious diseases – did nothing to hinder his precipitous fall.

Splat.

Poor Johnny.

However, his untimely demise did prove one unequivocal fact: no matter how much you try, you can never make everything safe. Not everything. It's a tumbledown, grubby, ramshackle, adventure-filled, and sometimes – yes, truly – dangerous world.

And... really... it's best left that way.

The Vampires of Windsor

Lily and Edward were an old couple. A very old couple. So very, very old, in fact, that some of the faded, dusty, long since out-moded paintings which hung everywhere in their little home had actually been painted while they were already old enough to be at work and not, as might have been imagined at first glance, a hundred or more years beforehand.

That old fireplace, too. It was Victorian, wasn't it? Same story. That had been installed by London Bespoke Fires Ltd at the direct request of Edward. And London Bespoke Fires Ltd had been bombed into dust during the Second World War.

The same thing was true of the sink in their kitchen, and the ceramics in their bathroom. That company, King's Tiled Goods, had also long since ceased to exist. And yet Lily, already in her twenties at the time, had ordered those fittings direct from the owner of King's Tiled Goods. In fact she had chosen them back in the day where you picked something out of a black and white hand-printed paper brochure, before then visiting a shop and placing an order in person. A brochure filled with all kinds of items which people had stopped using in the 1960s, if not many years earlier. Things like wrought iron mangles, copper bottomed boilers for cleaning clothes and other funny things like that.

So yes, Lily and Edward were a very, very old couple.

And they had lived in Windsor all their long lives.

In Windsor, and always in this one single house.

Never moving away, never wanting to move away.

All those years, spent in the same home. (Except for the odd holiday taken in rural Scotland).

True, the stairs now creaked a good deal, as they climbed them, slowly but capably enough, to bed every night. A good deal? Yes. But still a lot less than their old bones did.

And yes, their favourite armchairs, filled with horsehair and at least five times re-covered – the last by an upholsterer who was also long since dead – were now stained in a rather gruesome manner at head height, and also where hands had grasped the arms of the chairs so countless many times. But those stains were not due to any lack of cleanliness on Lily and Edward's part. Not at all – they were simply down to the fact that they had been using those same two armchairs since first acquiring them way back in 1952.

Even older, much of the hand-chosen wallpaper, for example on the stairwell in that impossible to reach and more-or-less wasted space above the stairs, was Edwardian in origin. Dating from the very end of that period, so about 1909, but Edwardian none the less.

And the same held true wherever a person went in their small terraced Windsor home.

Everything was old. And most of it was now, if not originally, one shade or another of brown.

"Who knew?" remarked a social worker after one visit with a colleague, "Who knew there were as many shades of brown as can be found in that one little house in Windsor?"

He and his friend had laughed a great deal about that, whilst studiously washing their hands before having a spot of lunch in the local cafe.

Why did they laugh so? Well, perhaps because of fear. They, none of them, liked to visit the house. There was, they all felt, *something* about it.

And *something* about the old couple, too.

Of course being old, even *that* old, was nothing to be ashamed about. Far from it. Life offers us all two basic choices: live to be a ripe old age like Lily and Edward, or die somewhat younger than that. And there it is. The full range of options for all of us. (Neither of which is particularly wonderful when you look at them in the cold light of day. Surely life could have been arranged so that we would live for 80 years and remain young for the first 75 of those? As things stand, life feels rather imbalanced and we are assuredly not young enough for long enough.) Thus being so very old, creaking a little, a lot, and living in a house full of brown things with stains here and there was just the way things were. More or less par for the course. For all of us.

Besides, plenty of young people today live far worse lives. Building up their weight as if there was going to be a food shortage any moment now, as if the supermarkets were all going to close down, as if all our major trading deals would disappear overnight, gobbling down stuffed crust pizzas every evening and washing them down with a litre or more of sugared drink. That was far, far worse than living to be ancient. At least this old couple had never done any of *that*.

And then there was the recent discovery of the sedate joys of 'online sport' (or computer games by any other name), which allowed other young people to increasingly take their own levels of inactivity to horrible new limits. The same folk who then wondered why they could not run for the bus even though they had yet to reach the age of forty. Who then collapsed and found themselves being ferried to hospital. A burden on the health system, into which, unlike the old, they have yet to pay their full amount. At least this old couple had never done *that*, either.

And, while we are on the subject, it's also important to remember that some old folk run marathons or do parachute jumps or go underwater and film sharks even as they approach their century. And they remain slim, eating proper home-cooked food all their days. Active and slim. So no, there's nothing intrinsically difficult or grim or grisly or brown about getting old. Quite the opposite really.

Only this couple.... well... no....

No.

The truth was that this particular (very) old couple really did have something else about them. Something altogether more sinister.

But what was it?

Well... some years earlier, a young female social worker had visited their home, to check on their health and well-being, to make sure they could afford tea and biscuits, could afford to have their fire lit for (at least, but not more than) three days a week in winter, stuff like that. And she had been politely invited to stay for a short while and share a cup of the aforementioned tea. (Though she got no biscuit. There were none of those to spare.)

The young social worker had checked her watch. She had no more visits to make that day, and so she had agreed to a cuppa. "Yes, why not?" she replied politely, folding her hands in her lap.

Now, as it happened, during this particular visit the old man was upstairs. So when Lily left the front room to go and make the tea, for a short while, the social worker was left quite alone to sit and wait.

And that was what she did.

Sat.

Waited.

A clock tick-tocking being the only audible sound.

She sat in that dimly lit, brown coloured parlour. She sat, she waited and she could not prevent her eyes from wandering from one object in the fussy little room to another.

So she saw some of those old paintings, and the sturdy old fireplace, and she also saw floral vases with long dry dead roses in them, brass ornaments no longer properly polished, an old TV which looked as if it had never been used, and a few other such knick-knacks. And then her eye fell upon a faded, sepia photograph, in a fine silver frame on the mantelpiece. She couldn't quite make out what the photograph was. So she got out of her chair, and took a few steps over to the picture to have a closer peek at it.

What she saw shocked her.

Very much so.

"Goodness me! It's her", she said, aghast. "I'm sure it is. That's Lily in that photo!"

The photograph was of an old lady, and a young man, standing in front of a Spitfire. Not a Spitfire in a museum, but a Spitfire ready to go into action, to shoot down some

Germans. That sort of Spitfire. A photograph which must, therefore, have been taken in about 1940.

"Oh, but it can't be", said the young social worker as she sat back down again. "No. It must be her grandmother".

At that moment, the old man, Edward, came into the room. He saw their visitor looking at the photo and nothing short of an evil glower flashed briefly across his face. A dark and horrible expression. But he managed to hide it before the social worker turned toward him.

"Ah" he said, his voice rather croaky, dusty, brown one might almost say. "I see you are admiring that photograph. Yes, indeed, it was taken during the last war. We all played our part".

He sat. He sat on the sofa directly opposite the visitor, to make sure he could keep an eye on her expression.

"Ah, yes", said the young lady coolly. "And I was just thinking how much your wife's grandmother, in the picture there, looks er... well, exactly like her".

The old man nodded. "Yes", he said. "There is a strong family resemblance, isn't there?"

Then the old lady, Lily, came back into the room with the tea. Which was served, and no more was said about the photograph on the mantelpiece. The social worker chatted away politely for a while, made sure the very old couple had all they needed or, at least, all they were going to be given, and then she made her excuses to leave.

It was a mere 24 hours later that a body was found floating face-down in the river Thames.

The body was that of a young social worker.

Of course no connection whatsoever was made between the visit of the social worker to the couple in Windsor and her untimely death in the Thames. A brief investigation by Inspector Metre of the Yard, found no reason whatsoever to suspect any foul play. Clearly the young woman had simply committed suicide, hitting her head, presumably, on the stone parapet on her way down to the river and her untimely end.

Social workers, after all, were prone to despair and depression. That came with the job.

And so the case was closed.

And life went back to normal.

But what was 'normal' in that little Windsor household?

It took another accident for Lily and Edward's secret to be discovered...

The tiny terraced house in Windsor had a cellar. (Of course it did.) And at the front of that cellar, in the garden, at ground level and almost completely hidden and long since forgotten about, was a rather attractive iron grille. The grille was for ventilation and perhaps to allow a bit of daylight down into the underground space, though precious little of that must have actually reached the cellar as the grille was now wholly hidden by a dense evergreen shrub of some sort and must have been that way for many a long year.

At some other point in its history – who knew when or why – a part of that same grille had also been broken. Broken just enough, in fact, to leave a small gap through which, should such a thing ever occur, a ball followed by a small dog might well be able to squeeze.

Needless to say, finally, on one bright day in the spring of 2021, such a thing did occur. As, indeed, do all things, sooner or later. And a ball bounced through the broken grille, thrown by a child who had just moved in next door, and followed by the above mentioned small dog.

The child, fortunately, saw where both had gone. She saw the dense evergreen shrub, she saw the ornate cast-iron grille behind it, she saw the ball disappear into the thing and she saw trusty Milly go determinedly after it. She saw all of that, so there was no chance of the dog being left trapped in the cellar. (No harm comes to animals in any of my stories!)

"Dad", said little Susie as she came back into their new home, where the old kitchen was being taken out and a big shiny silver and white one installed in its place and which, therefore, meant the kitchen was really quite a mess from top to bottom. "Milly has gone through a metal thing next door, into their cellar, and I can't get her out".

Her father was busy. Or, at least, he was trying to look busy so he could avoid having to help his wife deal with the builders, the demolition of the old kitchen and the installation of the new one.

"What's that? What do you mean? What metal thing?"

Susie explained.

"Oh, I see", said Dad. "Well then, I'd better leave your Mom to handle things here, and you and I had better pop around next door and ask the neighbours if we can go down to their cellar and rescue Milly then, hadn't we?"

And so that was what they did.

Dad and little Susie knocked on the front door of their very (very) old neighbours' house, and waited patiently, but got no reply.

Then they peered through the iron grille and called for Milly.

The dog replied with a small bark or two.

"She seems OK", said Dad. "But it doesn't look like anyone is in. So we will have to try again later".

But the daughter, with a much greater sense of what really mattered and what didn't, was having none of that.

"No!" she said. "I want to get Milly out now. It isn't fair to leave her in there, it was my fault the ball went through that stupid thing, not hers. So I have to get her back now!"

Susie was right, of course, and so the two of them tried knocking on the door again.

But there was still no answer.

"Well there's nothing we can do about it", said Dad grumpily. "The neighbours must be out and we will have to leave it until later".

"No, Dad", said Susie again. "I want to get Milly out now! We can't leave her down there. What if them old people don't come home until night-time or what if they have gone on holiday or something?"

Dad frowned.

"They must have a back door like us, Dad", said little Susie encouragingly. "We could always go in that way".

Dad was disinclined to do that. It would mean climbing over the garden fence and entering a stranger's house uninvited. But... on the other hand... it would keep him out of the kitchen, and it did seem wrong to leave Milly in the cellar. What if she was hurt?

So that was what they did.

First Susie and then, clumsily and awkwardly Dad, climbed the fence and, with a bit of hesitation, following another unanswered knock or two, they tried the back door.

It was unlocked. Invitingly so.

"Hello, is anybody there?" Dad called.

"Where is the cellar?" asked the little girl, getting to the nub of the matter without any of the dithering of an adult.

Dad called out again.

Twice.

But still there was no answer forthcoming.

And, by contrast, the door to the cellar was right there. Under the stairs. Exactly where the door to the cellar stood in their own house.

"Come on", said Susie, shoving with all a little girl's force on the seemingly stubborn to open old wooden door until it finally gave in and swung reluctantly ajar.

And with that, Susie, followed by Dad, went down into the cellar.

Milly was fine.

Even the rubber ball was unharmed.

But the cellar, or rather the contents of the cellar? Well, that was quite a different story.

Along one wall, lay two long wooden boxes. Wooden boxes with brass handles.

Both of these boxes had their lids on, and both lids were closed.

Dad took a quick glance at those boxes, recognised them immediately for what they were, and decided that it would probably be best for Susie and Milly (and even the rubber ball) to go back upstairs and return to their own home.

So Susie did that. She picked up her little dog and slammed the cellar door shut as she left, as she had always been told to do with doors.

Dad then spent a bit of time examining the rest of the contents of that strange and rather disturbing space.

It was a cellar. So of course there were thick cobwebs and stuff like patches of damp or whatever. And of course there was a rather strange foosty smell, too.

But what else was there?

Beside another wall, there was a table, a heavy one, very sturdy, with bottles on top, and tubes, a tangle of rubber tubes. He wasn't certain, but the bottles very much resembled those which blood donors use. And the stains on the table confirmed that these bottles too, may possibly have been used for such purposes. But why?

And what was that? Underneath an old (and also stained) towel, there was a pile of newspapers. Or, at least, a pile of cuttings from newspapers.

Dad picked them up. Blew a big spider off the topmost piece of paper and began to flick through them.

"Goodness me", he said. "Some of these things date back a full hundred years or more".

The light in the cellar was not at all good, but Dad's eyesight was excellent and there was just about enough natural daylight to allow him to read the less faded cuttings.

"Child goes missing in Windsor", read one newspaper. Dated 1926. "Seventh child disappears in the Thameside town. Mystery deepens...".

Just like the missing infant, the rest of that fragment was also missing. So he tossed that to one side and read a second scrap of paper.

"Two children disappear near the Thames, Windsor", said another. That was dated 1929. "Bodies found in water. Drained of..." and the rest of that was illegible.

Drained of? Drained of what?

And the other newspaper cuttings? He glanced at a few more of them.

They all told similarly disturbing and rather grisly stories.

"You know, I think I'd better call the police about this lot. There's something off about this little house in Windsor". said Dad out loud yet to himself.

Or, at least, he thought he was saying it to himself.

Because he didn't believe that anyone else was down in the cellar with him.

But there was someone else down there...

"Ahhhh! Thank goodness you are here, young man", said an awfully dry and croaky voice.

A woman's voice.

Dad turned around. And, sure enough, there was a very (very) old woman in the cellar with him.

"When that cellar door closes", she continued, "it has a terrible tendency to jam firmly shut, and simply cannot be opened from this side at all. A few weeks ago my husband and I forgot to prop it open, and so we were both rather stranded down here".

She coughed. A horrid rasping sort of cough.

"Though we were never so much hungry, as thirsty, you see", said the woman, her eyes widening to an unnatural degree as she looked at Dad. "So incredibly thirsty".

She stopped. And took a rather sad and mournful look at the second coffin which remained firmly shut.

"Ah! Poor noble Edward. Finally. My dear husband. After all these years together, forever at my side, how I shall miss him", she licked her thin, wrinkled lips. "Still, in the end, one of us had to make the sacrifice. And I can honestly say that he gave up his own life without too much complaint".

War without end

"Hello! Wake up!"

Slowly the tiny little old man turned over. But he didn't wake up. He mumbled a few words and went back to sleep.

The soldier straightened. Stood up.

Overhead the sun was out. The sky was blue. Piercingly, dazzlingly, blue. It would be yet another hot day.

Had he been elsewhere, had he been back home in England, which was where he longed to be, he would have loved days like these. Hot and sunny. With the right conditions, the right winds, he would have gone down to a beach with a few friends, all loaded up with surfboards. Then, later, a few beers and maybe one of the girls would bring them all some grub. A barbie on the beach.

What could be better? And how many times had he done that? And it had always been fun.

Fun. Fun? Yeah. It was funny how sun and sand, there and here, were the same... and yet so very different.

Here? He was sick and tired of the sun, day after day, so dry, remorseless. It killed everything. The landscape was bleached barren. Oh for some rain. But if the sun was bad, he was even more tired of the endless grating sand. It got everywhere. Truly. Everywhere. Despite wearing goggles almost all day, every day, his eyes were red raw from the biting sand. His lips were chafed. He drank sand in his water, ate sand in his food, it was inside his helmet, matted into his hair, down inside his boots, his clothes, everything. Everywhere. Truly. It got everywhere.

He sighed.

Shook his head.

Looked around.

There was no one else about. Nothing.

He was here, in this rubbled village, with another two soldiers from the same squad. The three of them had been dropped off to wait for another vehicle. The village itself was known to be safe, deep inside a safe area and, in all honesty Adam and the other two soldiers had expected to sit in the sun for an hour or so, seeing nothing, hearing nothing and probably taking it in turns to rest.

But the first thing to do was to have a quick look around the place.

Just to be sure.

Each heading in different directions.

In fact Adam had not gone very far before he had spotted a bundle of rags, lying in a heap beside a ruined house –rags, that in fact had turned out to be this old, old, old little old sleeping man.

At first he had thought the man to be dead. Yet one more pointless casualty of this seemingly endless war. But no. The man was alive.

He gently shook the figure again.

And once more the man mumbled a few words.

But still he didn't wake up.

Was there anything here apart from destruction? This wasteland of sand and sun.

A car sat in the middle of the road, broken in half and long since burned out, now mostly rust and sharp metal. Sand blasted too, of course.

A few houses or, to be exact, a few buildings which used to be houses, but were now piles of adobe rubble. But otherwise nothing.

Adam's tired eyes searched all over the place and saw... nothing. The village was silent. Whoever had been here, once, for whatever purpose, it seemed they had long since gone.

How he longed to be back home. Back on those Cornish beaches. So many years in his past. A life distant. Almost forgotten.

He sighed again, then bent down, once more, to the little wizened sleeping old man.

"Come on", he said. "Wake up now, please."

This time, the tiny glaucous eyes did open.

And the man started. Understandably enough, given that he had awoken to find a soldier in full desert battle gear standing over him.

It must, briefly, have been like waking *to* a nightmare, rather than waking *from* one.

No. Not briefly. No. It was actually waking to a very real nightmare. Because the whole world, the whole of this old man's world, had collapsed into war. There had been nothing but bombs, soldiers, destruction, noise and terror for years now. Years of hellfire interspersed with long periods of utter silence and emptiness. A horrible calm between storms, which in many ways felt worse than the fighting itself.

The man blinked. Then, slowly, awkwardly, he sat up.

"That's better", said Adam with a smile. "You're OK?"

The man must have been eighty years old if a day. Probably even older than that. And no bigger than a young child. His beard was frazzled and grey, resembling the tail of an alley cat who had seen better days.

The man spoke. In Arabic.

Then he corrected himself and spoke in surprisingly good English.

"Have you... have you some water?" said the man slowly. His voice as thin as a reed and as dry as old straw.

Adam nodded, producing a canteen of water and offering it to the man, who remained seated.

The man took the canteen, opened it, and sniffed at the contents.

Nothing to smell except lukewarm water.

"May I take it all?" said the old man.

It was the only water Adam had with him. But the others would have some too and, in any case, it should only be an hour or so before they were picked up. The man appeared as withered as could be. So yes, of course, if he needed the water, he could take it. All of it.

"Sure", said Adam. "Help yourself."

"Most kind", said the old man. "You are most kind." And with barely more than one gulp he had swallowed the whole bottleful. Quite visibly reinvigorated by the liquid. "Ah. That is better!"

"Wow", said Adam quietly. "I'm glad I found you. You must have been very thirsty."

The old man nodded. "I was. It had been too long since I last drank."

"Are you hungry, too?" said Adam.

The old man nodded again. "Yes, I believe yes. It has been very many years since I ate. If you have some food... then yes, please."

Adam didn't notice the word 'years' in that sentence. He didn't notice because life, during this war, was one long series of surprises – most of them unpleasant. And a soldier's eyes and ears soon learned to shut out irrelevant details.

"I don't really have any food", said Adam, patting his pockets. "Not really. Not proper food." But he did have an energy bar. "Though I've got this", he said, producing the thing from his pocket.

The old man peered at the foil-wrapped item as if he had never seen such a thing before. "Is this all you have?" said the old man. His voice now, quite markedly, stronger than before. "Like with the water?"

Adam nodded. "Yes. I'm afraid so. Sorry. But you can have it."

Nothing grew out here. Nothing prospered. There were no trees, no fruit, no vegetables. There must, once, have been goats or something like that, but they were long gone. This was empty, hostile, barren desert. A horrible place. Dry, hot and as harsh as could be.

Adam offered the energy bar to the old man, and the old man took it. Took it and, at first, clearly, had no idea what to do with it.

"Here", said Adam, taking the bar back and unwrapping it. "Now you can eat it."

And that was what the little old man did. He ate the bar in more or less one gulp.

And, just as with the water, as he swallowed the food, so he appeared to grow a little in size, strength, vigour and vitality.

"Ah!" said the old man. "That feels better. It has been too long."

For a moment neither of them spoke.

The silence of the desert is a deafening sound. A horrible sound. Quite different from the calm of a leafy wood on a sunny day. Quite different from the feel of a bed, with cotton sheets, at the end of a busy day. The silence of the desert is the silence of death. Or nothingness.

"Who are you, if I may be so bold as to ask that question?" said the old man, finally. "And why are you here?"

Adam laughed. Those were more or less the very questions he had been going to ask the old man.

"Sergeant Adam White", said Adam. "And as to what I am doing here, well that's a bloody good question."

The old man smiled too. He had understood the bitterness in Adam's answer. "You are far from home?"

Adam nodded. "I am. Too far. And for too long."

The old man nodded. "I see", he said.

"And you?" asked Adam. "If you don't mind."

The old man shrugged. "I have always lived here", he said. "But I have no home."

It was an odd reply. But Adam was too tired to worry about its meaning. "And your name?"

"Saloo", said the old man. "Or, at least, that is what I have so often been called."

"Well, Saloo", said Adam, "I'm sure you can come along with us, back to base, and we can sort things out for you a bit. Do you have anyone else here? I mean, friends or family or are you completely alone? The village seems to be completely deserted."

Saloo stood. And he was quite a bit taller than he had first appeared, when Adam had seen him curled up resembling a pile of rags.

"Oh no", Saloo replied. "I am quite alone. Quite, quite alone."

"You can come with us", Adam repeated the words, tiredly and almost in a monotone.

"Forgive me", said Saloo. "But here is where I live and where I must stay. I cannot leave with you. Nor do I wish to leave this place."

Adam could not have imagined anyone wanting to stay in the empty, battered, barren, sun blistered, sand-blasted village. But orders were orders. Villagers were never to be moved unless a zone was in combat or unless they wished to be moved. And as this village had long since ceased to see any fighting, and as Saloo had no wish to move... that was that. He could stay here.

Nevertheless, for some reason, just this once, despite having been in similar situations many times before, there was something, some nagging doubt within Adam, some concern, about leaving the old man alone here in this village. This barren place.

"Er... well..." Adam began. "If you're sure. But... do you have any water? Or food? I mean... you'd not eaten or...."

Saloo shook his head. "It is rare I need to eat or drink", he said quietly. "Once, a little, every now and then is sufficient for me."

Adam nodded.

He felt hot and tired.

The sand was starting to irritate his eyes.

"You gave me all your water?" said Saloo.

"Mmm", said Adam. "It's OK, no worries."

"And all your food?" said Saloo.

"Sure", said Adam.

"Then I shall give you one desire, one wish in return", said Saloo.

Adam shrugged. "Ah no. Don't worry about it. Your need was greater than mine. Anyway, we can get some more off my mates when they catch up."

Saloo nodded. "That is good you have friends. Here is a hostile place. Friends are good here. Do you mind if I ask you a question?"

"Go ahead", said Adam, wondering if they should go indoors, out of the sun, and not really focusing on what the old man was saying.

"If you could stay here or leave, right now, at this moment, which would you do?"

"Erm... what?" said Adam. "I'm sorry?" He laughed. "Leave. I'd leave."

"But your friends?" said Saloo.

"Oh they'd be alright", said Adam. "Survive anywhere, those two."

"Then you may leave", said Saloo. "That will be done."

Adam nodded. Very absent-mindedly.

"But I have another question", said Saloo.

Adam thought he heard his friends and turned to look, but there was nothing in the street. Just the wind blowing a scrap of litter into the rubble.

"Tell me", said Saloo. "Would you choose to be younger or older than you are now?"

"I'm sorry. What did you say?"

"Choose to be older or younger than you are now. It can be ten years. Either way. Which would you choose?"

The question seemed strange. But then... this was the middle of a war, a war that had already lasted almost exactly ten years. A war in a hostile place. In a desert. A war that seemed to have no real sense. So, truth be told, everything seemed strange.

"If I could choose to be older or younger?" said Adam slowly.

"Yes", said Saloo. "But take care! Few ever choose older. The lure of youth is great."

Adam laughed. "Well.. right now... If I could choose, I would definitely be younger. Back on one of those beaches in Cornwall, with my friends and..."

In the time it took to blink one of his rather red, tired and bloodshot eyes, Adam opened them again to find himself, or so it seemed, on a beach, with the sea crashing in front of him, the wind blowing wildly, surfboards all around, and friendly familiar faces on every side.

"Come on Adam", said Siobhan. "We're all waiting for you."

Adam instinctively bent down and picked up his red surfboard. And then ran with it, laughing, loving life, into the foaming blue water. His mind as clear and as fresh as sharp as it had always been. His body no longer tired. The sun and the sand feeling gorgeous once more.

"Where's Jack?" he shouted as he hit the first wave.

He disappeared into the water, which felt wonderful. Like life itself. Resurfacing to find happy smiling faces all around. Siobhan next to him in the water. Her dazzling white bikini matching her platinum blonde hair.

"Here he is!" someone else shouted.

And there, sure enough, just pulling up, in his old battered VW camper van, surfboard on top, was Jack. Adam's best friend. They had known one another since the age of five. Always at the same school, always in the same class.

"Jack!" Adam shouted, leaving the water behind and walking over to greet him, crossing the soft sand, running his fingers through his wet hair as he did so. "Where you been? We've all been wondering..."

Jack clambered out of the van, looking a little dazed and surprised. "Aww... sorry mate", he said as he shook Adam's hand. "I was held up a bit back at home". He hesitated. Maybe even, just briefly, looked a little pale. "I've only been bloody called up, haven't I?"

Adam froze. Hadn't he heard those very same words at least once before? "Called up? What? You mean... you mean you've been called up for that...". His voice tailed off.

Jack nodded. "Yeah. That business in the desert *has* all kicked off. I told you it would. So we're going over in a few days' time. And you too, chap. Your regiment has been called up, too. You and me will be going over together, I reckon."

"Come on!" It was Siobhan again, shouting from the water's edge. "Hurry up, you two! Stop hanging around. I want to see which of you make the best wave today".

Jack smiled, looked at the water, then shrugged. "Well. Who cares? So what if we do have to go over. It's only a bit of desert isn't it? Sun and sand. A war out there won't last forever, will it?"

Oddity

Oddity was.
And there was no denying it
Because Oddity simply was.

But what Oddity was,
that wasn't so easy to say.

Was Oddity that gap?
That horrible gap.
That great big gap between have n' have not.

Or was Oddity that other gap?
That chasmy gap.
The one between here n' being over there.

Well,
whichever Oddity was,
it was odd that Oddity still was it.
Because it was time that Oddity wasn't,
and that those gaps were not any more.

But the *real* oddity was not any of that, but
that nobody seemed to mind!
So whatever it was, Oddity still was it,
and saw it would not soon be left behind!

"I'm Oddity long the cause of so much trouble!"

"I'm Oddity the reason for so much pain!"

"I'm Oddity here to make misery".

"I'm Oddity and here to remain!"

Then one day, of a sudden, it all had stopped,
just as oddly as it all had started.
Things were given out and shared,
and Oddity it seemed had parted.

Was it some sense had been finally seen or
was it great big changes had been made?

Or was it just that even Oddity had bored with the
same old game?

Is statue?

The pavements and roads around Beddledere Square were very dark. Much darker than usual. In fact they were so dark it was almost as if someone, somewhere, had turned off all the street lights on purpose.

Which, of course, was exactly what someone *had* done.

Though only young, thanks to his family connections, Louis Timmings-Jones was already a senior manager at Orford County Council – a stepping-stone to elsewhere – and so it had been simplicity itself to persuade a few members of staff, much lower down the pay scale, that those street lights all needed to be off on the evening of Tuesday 12th March.

"All of them?"

"All of them", Mr Timmings-Jones had insisted.

And though the workers had their doubts and questions, worries and concerns, these they kept to themselves as, doing what they were told, they switched all the lights off and plunged Beddledere Square into pitch darkness.

The ubiquitous CCTV cameras, however, were a trickier problem. In most countries, even today, CCTV is limited to a few chosen or important sites. Banks may have them. Certainly indoors. Art galleries too. Things like that. Why so few places? Perhaps those other countries still feel that privacy is more important than surveillance? Or a degree of responsibility more important to society than knowing who dropped that empty beer can? Who can say. But whatever the reasons for the proliferation of these little electronic spies all across our Sceptered Isle, it did mean that certain actions were much harder to perform. (Though, of course, even the most rudimentary of fancy dress disguises would make all those endless hours of film more or less redundant. But that's for another story.)

Fortunately, one of Timmings-Jones' fellow conspirators, Matthew de Somers, though only in his early twenties, just happened to be a member of the same dining club as the chap who ran the company who owned most of the CCTVs in Orford – an organisation called Grope Five, who were also responsible for looking after single female travellers in various quarantine hotels. (But that's yet another story.) And so it was as easy as opening a third bottle of champers, to persuade that same man to turn off all the cameras, on one particular evening, for "routine server maintenance". After all, as Mr de Somers said, the whole thing was just one big wheeze. High jinks. Nothing more serious than that.

Lights out.

Cameras not rolling.

And so the scene was set.

The only remaining obstacle was to place a few 'Road Closed' signs at strategic points so that no passing police car could possibly come upon the scene by chance. Not, to be fair, that there was a great likelihood of a police car doing that, because on most nights, of course, they were *both* very busy at the local chip shop ordering ever more scarce supplies of sea fish.

Despite all those precautions, however, Timmings-Jones, de Somers and their comrades still spoke in whispers as the moment for action finally arrived.

"TJ", said Anna Haviland, in as quiet a voice as she could manage, being the sort who normally brayed like an angry donkey. "Are you set?"

"Set", replied TJ.

"Go, go, go", whispered Anna.

"Pardon?" said TJ.

"I said, 'Go, go, go'".

"Oh, OK. Righto".

And suddenly the pin-droppingly quiet Beddledere square burst into fifteen minutes of frantic and somewhat noisy activity.

From one corner, a large flatbed truck roared into life. Lights on, illuminating the whole place, driven by the two young men who saw the whole thing as a bit of a righteous caper. The truck screeched a little, as it left the road surface and rattled across the cobblestones, then crashed in a very un-ceremonious manner straight through the ornamental wrought iron railings which, of course, surrounded the stone plinth and statue in the very centre of the square.

And as this was all going on so, from the opposite direction, came a lumbering, thundering, JCB. (Loaned, of course, for the night, via the right family connections.) Anna Haviland drove this. And she drove it with a very visible fury, almost as if she, herself had been personally slighted by their stone target.

"Easy a bit", said Margaret Biddlewhite, her co-driver for the night. "I'm sure you just ran over a cat or something".

"Bah!", said Anna. "Nothing is going to stop me, not now".

Margaret looked back over her shoulder. "Oh, it's alright. It was only a dustbin", she laughed.

And upon that news, Anna put her foot down all the harder – not that a JCB can go all that fast – and the machine rattled and rolled and shook the air even more than before. Especially as it, too, reached the cobblestones.

The statue, on the plinth, and the goal of that night's attack, was none other than the famous colonialist author Howard Perceval.

Mr Perceval, born 1830 and died... no-one knew quite when, had been standing in Beddledere Square for the last 100 years or so. Or, at least, his statue had been standing there for all of that time. It – the statue – had been erected by the Christian Indian Society of Orford university. Back at a time where it was considered proper to bring Christianity to people loosely named Indians, and equally proper to relate accounts of those same people in the most deprecating and patronising if not downright racist language.

Mr Perceval, one such Christian adventurer, had been hugely popular in his day, with some of his novels even being serialised in the mainstream press. And as his wealth had grown, he had often been invited to speak at places like Orford about his travels and adventures in "dark lands" amidst "backward folk".

Most of his tales were of the jaw-dropping sensationalist 'Can you believe that these people actually lack proper clothes' type. Occasionally, especially where the subject was a woman, backed up with lewd illustrations.

But others, of the type the Christian Indian Society preferred not to focus on, were about legends, myths and magic in those far-off lands.

Although a big, burly, handlebar-moustached sort of fellow, whenever Perceval spoke about those other, stranger adventures, many observers noted that he changed slightly, in delivery and possibly even appearance. Becoming, so it seemed to them, that little bit more cold, that little bit more grey, that little bit slower with every word he uttered.

This all went on for some time, until around the turn of the century, and scheduled to deliver yet another hot-air-filled account of how the third-world poor lived, to a packed audience of Orford types, Mr Perceval failed to appear.

And when looked for, at home and elsewhere, no trace could be found of him.

This was odd. Very odd. Not least because Perceval had never missed a chance to talk to people before, but also because he had only just set-up a scholarship for promising Orford students to travel across the globe and find as many uncontacted peoples as possible and take photographs of them and give them the good news about Christianity – whether they wished to hear it, or not. (Hence why the Christian Indian Society took him so readily to their bosom.)

But time passed.

Weeks became years.

And no one had any news of Perceval. He had, quite simply, disappeared without trace.

Eventually, keen to get their hands on his money, or, as they put it, "looking for a termination to this tragic business", his surviving kith and kin pushed for the obituary to be written and published.

And so it was, in The Times, only one week later.

And that, until the statue was erected a few years down the line, was the last anyone heard of Mr Howard Perceval.

His writing, justifiably, soon fell out of fashion. It was, in no uncertain terms, of its epoch. And it reflected very badly on that epoch.

But the scholarship, his scholarship, remained, and every year, a suitably wealthy white male took the money and had a fine old time visiting the remotest parts of our globe.

"Let's have that rotter off there!" cheered Louis Timmings-Jones, in a voice not exactly loud because somewhere inside he was still concerned about being caught, but just about loud enough to be bravely heard.

Margaret and Matthew cheered too. In the very same way. As did Jonas St-John Walker, Harry Chappings and Simon Villeford. Indeed the whole 'posse' had turned up to witness this event. (Although Simon had arrived rather late and still dressed in a dinner jacket. And the others were a bit cross with him about that. It wasn't just the lateness; they also felt that his attire rather let the side down.)

And with all that encouragement, not exactly ringing in her ears but certainly egging her on somewhat, Anna Haviland swung the JCB into position. The great iron jaws of the machine now sitting immediately in front of the statue of the offending novelist. (And colonial racist.)

"Ready!" she screamed. Quite forgetting the risk of being discovered.

"Ready!" said Louis.

"Tally Ho!"

"Go for it" said Margaret.

And so she did.

There was a brief and rather awful grinding sound, as the granite statue was demobbed from its plinth in one extremely heavy chunk, and then a terribly loud crash, as the jaws of the JCB swung the thing around so that it hung directly above the truck and then, in an instant, released the statue onto the flat bed of that vehicle.

"We've got him!" shouted Jonas and Matthew almost in unison.

Who knew it would be so easy to take down a statue?

What an achievement!

"But what's that though?", said Simon, picking up a roll of thin paper, crisp and brown, like a parchment, which appeared to have fallen from the bottom of the statue and landed on the now deserted plinth.

"Looks like a dirty old five pound note", said Harry. "Must have been stuck under the statue or something".

Simon shook his head. "No. I don't think so. It came from... it seemed to fall from the statue... like from inside it. And anyway, old five pound notes were white. Not crisp and brown".

"Oh who cares what it is! Let's get out of here!" said Margaret.

"Yes", agreed Louis. "Let's get gone before the rozzers show up!"

Of course getting the truck away, loaded up as it was, with young men and women and a large heavy statue, was easy enough.

The same, however, could not be said of the JCB. At the best of times it was slow, ponderous and noisy and so, sure enough, the police stopped Anna driving the thing away before she had even got as far as the adjacent Queens Square.

But that had been a price the 'posse' had expected to pay. The arrest of one of their members, the driver of the JCB. And, indeed, that was part of the reason Anna had volunteered to undertake that role.

Prison did not scare her.

Not one bit.

"Do what you like with me, officer", she said, as they did what they liked with her and loaded her into a police van. "I'll never squeal".

And nor did she.

The rest, however, were clean away.

And the truck roared off into the night with its somewhat unusual load, back axle complaining as it drove along and very much threatening to collapse under the massive strain.

Fortunately for the statue conquerors, their destination was only a couple of miles outside Orford, where Jonas St-John Walker's father had a pretty substantial estate.

"Here we are", said Jonas, "Better take it easy over the cattle grids though, what. We don't want to lose the old fellow now!"

Everyone laughed.

The estate itself, of course, had been built on the back of generations of poor British workers, not to mention the wars and thievery of the middle-ages, where siding with the correct monarch had given substantial rewards for some.

But none of that seemed to matter to Jonas or any of the others. The families of several members of their group had a cupboard or two full of such ancestral skeletons, but their own statues and paintings of highly suspect forebears were, for some reason, not considered to be as reprehensible as poor old Howard Perceval.

"Where to, old chap?" Louis asked. "West barn or the stables?"

"Oh the stables", Jonas replied. "I've set them up as a sort of studio, you know. We can store the statue in there and take our time deciding what to do with it".

"Deciding what would be the *funniest* thing to do with it, you mean!" added Margaret.

The whole mission had been planned to coincide with Jonas' father being away for a few months in the Bahamas, making sure his tax affairs remained nobody's business but his own.

And his mother, bless 'er, was never fully sober from one day to the next. So they probably could have put the statue in her bedroom and she wouldn't have noticed. (Indeed that very idea had crossed Jonas' mind but the thought of hauling the heavy weight all the way up the grand staircase, quickly ruled it out. And so the stable block would be used instead.)

"Are you OK, Simon?" It was Harry who asked the question. "You seem awfully quiet".

Simon, who the others assumed was sulking because of being told off for his late arrival and dinner jacket, nodded. "Fine", he replied. "I'm fine". Which, clearly, he was not. Something was bothering him, but what?

"Swing it out", said Louis.

The statue was promptly lifted clear of the truck and lowered gently down.

Here, having the original JCB already impounded could have caused a problem. How would the statue be removed from the truck and sited in the stables? But Jonas had foreseen such an eventuality, and had made sure that another such earth-moving machine was already at hand. (They really are pretty easy things to acquire, if you have the right connections.) And with a bit of careful manoeuvring and the odd moment of swearing, the statue was safely stashed inside the old stable block.

Stashed and set on a heavy duty wooden pallet, and quickly covered with a dark green and paint spattered tarpaulin.

"Oh how wonderful!" said Matthew.

"We've done it", said Harry.

"Such a shame Anna couldn't be here too celebrate our success, though", said Margaret.

"We'll pull a few levers and get her out tomorrow morning", said Louis. "Don't worry".

"All inside for champagne, I think", said Jonas. "It's all laid on. And a cold buffet too".

"Hooray!"

And into the stately home they all went.

All except for Simon. The youngest of the bunch and still, thanks to skipping a year or two, at university.

"Ah", he said, "Not me, thanks. I'll er... I think I'll give it a miss, if it's all the same".

The others thought his behaviour odd. But waved him off happily enough in a hastily arranged taxi.

The business of the night was over. It was clearly time to party.

Simon Villeford was a fully committed member of the 'Posse', of that there could be no doubt.

He had whole-heartedly supported a number of previous missions, mostly undertaken whilst the gang were all still at university. Of the six, even suggesting some of their more radical wheezes.

But where the rest had now gone out into the world, and were all managers of this or that company, or positioning themselves to become something big, he had disappeared for two years, ostensibly on protracted sick leave, but in reality taking that time out to travel around the world and live a little.

And whilst most of his experiences had been safe, expensive and clean, he had also encountered some real poverty and the odd smattering of harsh reality.

And that had changed him. A bit.

Certainly it had *begun* to change him.

In fact the dinner he had been attending was a charity affair. (Not that he had told the others that.) And he had even started to take his studies more seriously. So much so that he was beginning to have second thoughts about some of the gang's ideas. Did it really make sense to tear down a statue? To make such a big thing of the ignorance and racism of our colonial past whilst, in our own day, in our own country, men and women, children too, regardless of race or gender, were losing their homes, struggling to pay electric bills and resorting to food banks for basic nourishment? Wasn't the whole statue thing a terrible waste of time, effort, focus and energy? Indeed, was it any better than burning books one disagreed with? Of course Perceval and the others were wrong. Of that there could be no doubt. But wasn't it better to learn from that rather than make such a palaver about events that belonged to a different time...?

He wasn't sure.

And as he sat in his study room just after 3 a.m. he rightly decided that now was probably not the best time to try to puzzle out the answers to such difficult questions.

Instead, he recalled that odd piece of parchment.

The small scrap of paper he had picked up from the plinth of the statue, and stuffed without very much thought, into his trouser pocket.

What was it exactly?

"It's definitely got writing on it, as I thought it had", said Simon as he peered at the paper. "Is that Greek? Yes. Yes, I think it is. Had it been Latin I would have been able to read it. But Greek? No. That was never my strong point".

He tried his best to make sense of it, but the only word he was more or less certain about was 'marble' or perhaps 'stone'.

"I'll take it to Dr Jenkins tomorrow. He may be a history buff, but he speaks Greek as well as anyone".

And with that thought in mind, Simon yawned, stretched and decided it was time for bed.

Whilst Simon slept, the others, back at the estate, partied.

The champagne went down a treat. So much so that a fresh case had to be brought up from the cellars.

The cold buffet also went down a treat. Only for one or two of them, with all that champagne, and the excitement of the night, it also came back up a treat too.

"Gosh", said Jonas, "I'm simply too thrilled to even think of hitting the hay".

"Me too", said Margaret. "But I really cannot drink any more fizz".

"I have it!", said Louis. "Let's go to the studio and take a look at the old boy".

"Oh yes!" they all agreed.

"We should take some charcoal or paint or something, and see if we can't give the old fellow some colour!" laughed Louis.

"All already there, chum", said Jonas. "I've had bucket loads of paint delivered and stashed out there. So it's already a veritable artist's studio!"

And so, somewhat the worse for wear, the four remaining friends went out to the stable block. Crossing the dark courtyard, under a moonless sky, tittering and giggling as they went.

"What larks", said Jonas. "What larks!"

*

"Stone I am. Stone I became. I made myself this heavy way. And until a... time, is that? Time? Yes, until a time where others appear as foolish as I... Though foolish is very much a modern translation, the precise term did not exist in ancient Greece, of course. Stone I am. Stone I shall remain. Yes. Yes. I think that's about it, barring the odd tense perhaps. A more or less literal and accurate rendering, I should say", said Dr Jenkins, peering over the top of his glasses at the faded piece of parchment.

"Stone I am, stone I became?"

Dr Jenkins shrugged. "I'm afraid I can't help you with any of that, as things stand. But that is what it says".

So what did it all mean?

Simon scratched his head in thought.

"Could you give me a little more context, perhaps?" said the Doctor.

"Well..." began Simon slowly, "Yes.. I suppose a little, if it will help".

It was already mid-afternoon. Simon had slept like a log after the adventures of the previous evening. And it had taken him until now to cross the town to the college where Dr Jenkins taught.

Luckily the good doctor had not been too busy to see him.

"You must have heard of that statue being removed last night? That awful adventurer and novelist. Did you hear someone stole it? Took it down? The old colonialist so-and-so...."

Doctor Jenkins nodded. "Yes, yes, indeed. An awful fellow. But the statue thing? Well... rather a charade, in my opinion. But why? What does that have to do with this... erm...?"

"Well..." Simon lied slowly, "I happened to walk past the place this morning, where the statue had been, and there on the plinth, in amongst shards of stone, which appear to have been chipped off the thing, I found that... note. Whatever it is. Couldn't make any sense of it. My Greek not being all that..."

The old historian nodded his head slowly.

"On the plinth, eh? Well, well, well. 'Pon my soul. That explains something then. If you happen to believe in all the old legends of course".

At those words, for some reason he would have been unable to explain, Simon felt a cold shiver run along the full length of his spine.

A long, icy, trickle, like cold water running slowly, very slowly, down his back.

"Legend? Oh, really? What... what legend?" he managed to ask, whilst trying his hardest to feign disinterest.

"Oh, you know how those things are", said Dr Jenkins dismissively. "Adventurer travelled the world, mixed with indigenous peoples, dabbled in the black arts, their black arts. All that kind of thing".

Simon shook his head.

Slowly.

An unmistakable sense of dread now growing inside him.

"No... er.. what then was...er.. this... erm legend", he stammered. "What is it?"

"Well", the historian frowned, "As I recall it, Perceval, Howard Perceval, simply disappeared one day. No one could find hide nor hair of him. He was supposed to show up and ramble on, as per usual, at some talk or other, but he didn't show. And from that day on, no one ever saw him again".

Was that the full legend?

"Oh no, no. They also believed at the time that the fellow had been dabbling in dark arts, as I said. And that as a result of that he had been ageing or, rather going grey and getting slower and slower, heavier and heavier, rather like the Dorian Grey story. As if the life was slowly being sucked out of him by something or other. All rather gruesome, to be honest. And then, of course, that er... that society... the Christian Indian Society, I think it was, they wanted to honour the man with a statue. They rounded up a whole lot of funds for doing exactly that, but, so the story goes, they never spent it. Kept it. Had a nice big party or two instead".

Simon frowned at that. "What... No. Ah, but that bit can't be true, can it? Because they *did* put up that statue of Perceval. Very lifelike it was too".

Dr Jenkins shook his head. "Oh no. No, no. Apparently they found that statue of Perceval in his home. The fellow's own home. Standing right in the middle of his study, of all things. Imagine that? How utterly vain. Summed the man up, really. Still, as you say, whoever had carved it... they did a lovely job. An incredible likeness, by all accounts".

But Simon was no longer listening.

He offered a rather brusque thank you to the doctor and made his excuses to get away as quickly as possible.

Racing down the stairs and out of the college grounds.

"Stone I am, stone I will remain... yes. Until others just as foolish come along. Oh my Goodness! That was us. We were being just as blasted foolish".

He dashed across the road. Making his way to the nearby taxi rank.

"I must tell the others. Must warn them".

The taxi rank, however, stood empty. And it took a while for a vehicle to arrive.

Long enough, in fact, for Simon to begin to calm down.

And as the cab trundled slowly through the busy traffic of Orford, before finally reaching the country lanes, Simon began to laugh.

"What am I saying?" he said to himself. "Legends and black arts. I'm overtired. I've been studying too much philosophy".

The taxi finally arrived at the gates to the sprawling estate.

"This the place, guvnor?" said the taxi driver.

"Yes. Yes", said Simon. "Thank you. You can stop here, at the gate, save you going up the drive. I'll walk the rest of the way".

That walk fully and definitively settled Simon's mind.

The day was rather pleasant.

The birds sang. Spring was in the air.

He would be seeing his friends in a minute. And then they could all decide what to do about that blasted lump of granite or whatever it was.

"Wait till I tell the others about all of this", he chuckled. "They'll rib me, that's for sure. But...well.. there it is".

He arrived at the big house and waited patiently for someone to answer the door.

But nobody came.

Then he remembered Jonas' father was away in the Bahamas, and that his mother had 'issues' with alcohol.

"Oh, they'll all be in the stables", he said at last. "Of course. It's almost dinner time. I hope they haven't already painted it or something..."

Simon need not have worried.

The others were indeed in the stables.

But they hadn't done a thing to the statue.

Nothing at all.

In fact, they hadn't moved a muscle for very many hours.

And when Simon entered the building, the only living person he met was a large and strangely familiar man. A man with very old period clothes and a big, big, bushy handlebar moustache.

And beyond him, beyond the man, who had a very dark and unpleasant expression on his face, sat four small statues. And, somehow, they all seemed strangely familiar too.

Greedy pigs

The carbuncle was gone.

Once the great bold future, bright sunlit uplands, the vast concrete eyesore had finally been taken down.

Wind tunnel gone. Vandal city gone. Dark underpasses gone. Faceless inhuman monolith, no more.

But what to replace it with? Evidently the grand old town of Reekie needed a bold, new idea. Something wonderful.

The planning committee had three options in front of them.

First, there was a scheme to replace the carbuncle with an open space, a natural space, trees and greenery. There would be some buildings in there, too. Wooden ones. A small wooden theatre, to be used by local schools. A wooden cafe, to sell affordable, locally produced food. Seating lit with solar lights. Things like that.

Second, there was a plan to replace the great concrete whitlow with more shops, and bars, and a library, and a gym, but this time to build them out of brick and stone. On a very human scale. No building higher than three storeys. No great sheets of plate glass. An open car park, too, with reduced rates for local people. (After all, this was *their* city.)

Third, and finally, there was a new monstrosity. A great ugly concrete pile of nonsense. A thousand hotel rooms. A thousand hideously expensive studio flats and penthouses, all crammed in together but given posh sounding names and tiny little balconies to make them feel as if they something which they most certainly were not. Another vast faceless shopping centre, another inhuman wind-tunnel, lots of security features and none of it designed to blend in with the old town centre.

The planning committee duly considered all three choices.

Well... they huffed and they puffed and then, finally, they came to their inevitable conclusions.

The first plan was no good, they agreed, because a green space would surely encourage people to sit around with their shirts off and have fun and play football and do noisy out of control things like that. And, besides everyone knew that people would vandalise a park, given half an opportunity. Dogs would go to the toilet. Shocking. Children would get muddy. Pull up the flowers. No, no, that wouldn't do. No.

And so they moved on to the second plan.

The second plan was no good either, they agreed, because people surely wanted to shop in airless, modern, security-conscious malls now, and not in old-fashioned brick buildings oozing charm and character? A mall meant drive in, drive out. No exercise required. Fast fat food. And, anyway, providing things for local people wouldn't bring in any real investment would it? Not *real* investment. And that was what mattered. Even if they weren't quite sure what such a thing actually meant...

Inexorably they moved onto the third idea.

As for that? Well, it was another eyesore. Yes. And it was the most expensive option. True. It offered nothing of use to anyone local. Not really. And it was simply replacing one pile of nonsense with another. On top of which the developers were from overseas, the architects from down south (or another planet, it was hard to be sure which) and everyone concerned with the project was also helping themselves to tens of millions of pounds in taxpayers' money. But... on the other hand... to be fair... the third plan did come with brown envelopes very heavily stuffed with money. And so the planners decided to go ahead with that scheme.

After all, who cared if it was a scandalous waste of public money and something which would scar the city centre for another 30 years or so? By the time the next demolition came around, another planning committee would surely see better sense...

Mask masque

Everywhere Robert went that day, and everything he did, the result was more or less the same.

Well, not quite everything, because the day had started well enough.

Started like any ordinary day.

At 7 o'clock the alarm rang. Ten minutes later, it rang again. And five minutes or so after that, Robert hauled himself out of bed and ran into the bathroom.

The same story every morning.

He loved his sleep and had found it hard to get out of bed promptly ever since leaving school.

Back then, in his childhood, the alarm had always gone off at 7.30 a.m. And he had always, always, managed to get up within a few seconds of the ringing. Not once, in fact, in his whole 13 years at school had he been late. Not one single time.

Then he had left school. And for the earlier start at work, he needed to adjust his body clock by a mere half an hour. But no. He'd never been able to make that little change.

And as a result of that, more often than not, he arrived late for work. Often only a few minutes, but late all the same.

One of his friends, a windbag know-it-all sort, had insisted that all Robert needed to do was go to bed half an hour earlier.

But that hadn't worked.

The same windbag had then suggested altering the clocks in the house by half an hour and, in addition, going to bed 30 minutes early.

But that hadn't worked either.

Sleep with the window open?

Sleep with your feet in the fridge?

Nope. None of it worked.

Finally Robert had decided not to listen to the know-it-all any more, and whilst that didn't stop him arriving late for work, it did help. A bit. It helped in as much as Robert no longer had to listen to the dreadful fellow.

Today, however, was one of those days where, for no explicable reason, Robert would (probably) have arrived on time.

He ate breakfast at the normal speed.

He chopped and changed his clothes a few times, unsure of what to wear, just as he always did.

And he refused, as ever, to run for the bus even though as he turned the corner of Ealing Avenue, he could see that it was already standing at the bus stop.

But that refusal to run wasn't born out of stubbornness, however. It was a decision reached from many years' experience of public transport: if the driver sees you running, he will pull away from the bus stop. The only way, the only hope, to catch a bus already at a stop, is to make it look like you aren't interested in catching the thing at all. It isn't a fool proof approach. But sometimes it works. And today was, or would have been, one of those days.

One of those days where it worked.

Robert strolled up to the bus, expecting it to pull away at any moment, which would mean yet another late arrival for work, but with every step he took, the bus still refused to move.

Finally, only a couple of metres short, even Robert could not resist the urge to run, or at least jog, and wave his arm to catch the eye of the driver.

Did that do the trick?

Yes. The driver saw him, waited and the bus doors remained open.

"Phew" said Robert, as he hopped onto the bus, "I've made it".

He rummaged around in his pockets and, finally, found his bus pass.

He showed it to the driver. But the driver simply shook his head.

"You can't get on here mate, not without a mask".

Robert was stunned.

It was Wednesday, and he had caught the bus to work, and back home again, on both Monday and Tuesday, with none of those four trips requiring him to wear a mask.

"Ah... but...I always...".

"Sorry mate", said the driver again. "Put a mask on. Or you'll have to get off the bus".

"But.. I haven't got one of those masks", said Robert.

The driver simply shrugged.

Robert turned and looked along the crowded bus, and sure enough every face, normally so varied, the smiles, the frowns, talking, and so forth, every face was masked. People sat and stared, expressionless. More or less.

"You'll have to get off then", said the driver. "I've got a timetable to keep to, you know".

"Er... but do we really need... I mean... after all, if everyone else is wearing one... then I can't catch anything, can I? Nor can I give them anything? Surely?"

"Sorry mate", said the driver again. "Rules are rules. No mask. You'll have to walk".

And that, of course, as Robert had no mask, was exactly what he did. What he had to do.

Fortunately for Robert, it was a rather pleasant morning. And so he had no need to return home and grab a coat or anything like that.

And so he set off, following the bus route, making his long but not-so-very-long-really-in-the-scheme-of-things way to work.

"Bloody daft rules", he said to himself, more than once, as he walked along. "If I'd known about that, I'd have gotten up earlier".

Which, of course, he would not have done.

A short while later Robert reached the High Street, still ten minutes or so from his office.

The High Street was a perfectly ordinary sort of High Street. It had pawnbrokers' shops, lots and lots (and lots) of fast food outlets, a bookies or three, a couple of insurance agencies, at least five estate agencies and, at the far end, a proper old-fashioned sort of cafe. Which was open.

And as Robert reached the cafe, the walk making him hungry, the smell of cooking hungrier still, he realised for the first time ever, that his usual cup of coffee and chocolate bar was a pretty insubstantial breakfast.

"Blast", he said to himself. "I'm starving, now. This walk has not only made me late, but bloody hungry".

Then he had a bright idea.

"Wait a minute...." he said. "If I am already late, what harm would it do if I stopped off at the Kosy Korner Kafe and had a bacon sandwich or something?"

He was right about that, of course. If you are already late, then there is no more need to hurry. Not unless you are late for something extremely important – and no office job is ever *that* important.

So Robert decided to pop into the cafe and grab a bite to eat.

"Phew" said Robert, as he stepped into the warm and welcoming atmosphere of the cafe, "I'm glad you're open, I'm proper famished".

He walked towards the counter, smiling all the way, and patting his pockets as he did so to make sure that he had his wallet with him.

"Now... what shall I have?" he said as he read the menu, which was written in chalk on a blackboard just above the hot plates sizzling busily with sausages, eggs and bacon.

"I'm sorry", said the bald-headed owner of the cafe, "But you can't come in here mate, not without a mask".

Robert was stunned. Again.

He had used the cafe only last week, and he'd had no mask then. Nor had any of the other customers, not back then, not as far as he recalled anyway.

"Ah, yes... but...I've got to... I missed my bus...".

"Sorry mate", said the proprietor again. "Put a mask on. Or you'll have to leave, I'm afraid".

"But.. I haven't got one of those masks", said Robert.

The owner simply shrugged.

Robert turned and looked at the other diners in the cafe (or kafe) and noticed that every one of them was wearing a mask whilst waiting for their fried food to arrive and one, who had been served, was even squeezing a sausage into his mouth, around the side of his mask. That went down OK, the sausage. But when he tried to do the same thing with his fried egg... it made a terrible mess.

"You'll have to leave then", said the bald man. "I've got other customers waiting".

Which was true. There was already a queue behind Robert. Mostly overweight, that was also true, but a queue all the same. And they all wore masks.

"Yeah... but... if you try and eat with one on, it's impossible", said Robert, indicating the man with the egg.

The owner tutted. "Well, that's just daft, that is", he said. "Of course you can take them off to eat".

Robert frowned. "Eh? But... surely.. then what's the point of wearing them at all, if you take them off to eat? I mean, won't you spread germs then? Or catch..."

Once more the cafe owner shrugged. "Them's the rules, mate. The rules. There's nothing I can do. If you ain't got a mask, you can't order food".

And so Robert left the cafe and continued his walk to work. Hungrier than ever now that he had been within scoffing distance of the lovely fried food.

"Oh well", he said to himself, "I'll get a bit of something from the canteen before I go up to my office. It's only a few minutes from here".

Sure enough, three minutes later, there in front of Robert was the squat and rather ugly office block where, for the last three years, he had been working.

He glanced up at the large garish sign high up on the seventh floor and shook his head.

'OFFCRAP'.

It was one of those government quangos that was supposed to protect consumers' rights but which didn't really do very much in that respect, but which did, however, employ lots of people to push paper around in circles.

In this particular case, and to give them their full name, the quango was actually the 'Office or Clamping Regulations and Parking Regulations' or OFFCRAPR for short. But the last letter R had fallen off the sign in a storm last winter. And still no one had gotten around to issuing the paperwork required to replace it.

"Another day, another dollar", sighed Robert to himself.

And with that, he went into the building, aiming straight for the canteen.

OFFCRAPR was a more or less useless organisation. It failed to regulate clamping, and it failed equally to regulate car parking charges and the like. In part that was because the head of OFFCRAPR also owned a chain of multi-storey car parks, and in part it was because he had six other directorships, and all of them paid much more than this one. So he was never here. And he didn't care. And as a result of that, nothing ran smoothly and much of the quango scarcely ran at all. The whole place was dusty, quiet, inept, often almost empty and positively sleepy.

So it came as quite a surprise to Robert when, before he had taken even half a dozen steps into the building, an officious looking woman stopped him dead in his tracks with a barked "No" and a hand gesture to match.

"I am sorry, Sir", she said, standing square in front of Robert, and porting a bright blue mask as she spoke the muffled words, "But you can't come in here without a mask".

Robert was dumbstruck. It was the same story yet again.

"New orders, Sir", the woman continued. "All government buildings are to be closed to the public, except in emergencies".

"But...but... ah..." stammered Robert.

"I'm sorry sir", said the woman again. "But if you don't leave immediately, I will have to call the police".

"But... but I'm not a member of the public", Robert finally managed to blurt out. "I work here! On the second floor. My name is Mr Roberts".

The woman peered hard at him.

"You work here, sir?"

"Yes", said Robert Roberts.

"Oh, I'm very sorry sir. I didn't realise. I've only just started here myself today. New. Keen. Keen as mustard, Sir. You understand".

Robert smiled. "Oh, that's OK", he said. "It doesn't matter. Forget about it".

And with that he took another step.

"Oh no, Sir", said the woman, resorting to her barking tone once more. "You can't come in here sir, not without a mask. Like mine."

"But I work here!" said Robert.

"Makes no difference, sir", said the woman. "New orders, Sir. All employees, except senior management, bless 'em, must wear a mask inside government buildings at all times".

"But... but I haven't got a blasted mask like that!" snapped Robert. Getting pretty fed up with the whole thing by now.

"Sorry sir", said the woman. "Then you can't come in to work today".

Now as things would happen, it was at this very moment, and hearing that singular sentence, that Robert's immediate boss came out of the canteen.

Red faced and flushed, not least because the canteen had run out of jam doughnuts, so he would have to have his morning coffee without one, he glanced up at the clock and saw that Robert was already almost an hour late.

"What exactly is going on here?" he snapped.

"They won't let me into work", Robert replied.

"Why not?"

"Because I haven't got one of those stupid masks".

"And what do you propose to do about that?" asked his boss in a very unfriendly tone.

"I don't know...", said Robert, which, to be fair, was the truth. "I guess... Go home, I guess".

"Home?" growled the boss.

"I've got no choice" said Robert.

"Right. Then don't bother to come back tomorrow either. Masked or otherwise. You're always late. And now this. You're fired, my lad!"

And that was that.

Robert tried to protest, of course, but as the woman pointed out to him, protestations could not take place on government property unless the protestors were wearing masks.

So out he would have to go.

"What a day", sighed Robert to himself, as he sat on a park bench and reflected back over the events of the morning. "No bus, no cafe, and now no job. And all because I haven't got one of those silly masks".

Robert wasn't the kind of person to give up that easily, however. And he quickly formed a plan to take his dismissal to a tribunal. Right there. Right then.

"That's what I'll do", he said. "I'll call in at the Citizens Advice Bureau, right away, and tell them that I have just been unfairly sacked. They'll be sure to help me!"

So he left the park, and walked to the Citizens Advice or CAB.

Sadly, they too had just that very morning brought in a policy whereby no visitors were allowed into their building unless they were wearing an appropriate mask. However, the CAB were nothing if not helpful. And the notice pinned to their door also stated that, in the event you need urgent help but had no mask, you could call them. Use the telephone.

"I'll phone them then", said Robert.

Unfortunately, Robert quickly realised that his mobile phone was in his desk, in his office, back at work. So he couldn't call them.

"Oh, this is getting ridiculous", said Robert.

As indeed it was.

And so he returned to the park bench and sat down once more and formulated another plan.

"I know what I'll do", he said, "I will go home, now, stop off at the supermarket on the way and grab some food and drink to cook myself a nice dinner, and then I'll get straight on the computer and look for another job. I never liked that other one back there anyway". He paused. "And I might even order myself some of their daft masks too. So when I get my new job, they won't be able to turn me away".

Which, to be fair, did make sense given how hard life had become without one of those things.

So Robert set off from the park, feeling a bit better about his life, and walked the even longer way home via the supermarket.

Needless to say, any plans for the good dinner and maybe a glass or two of beer, soon went down the pan. Because a huge sign on the supermarket door, and an even bigger security guard, made it very clear that no one would be allowed in to buy food unless they were wearing a mask.

"Oh for goodness' sake", said Robert. "This is impossible. You've got to let me in. You can't refuse people the basics of life like food!"

"Sorry, Sir", said the burly security guard. "Policy is policy".

"Yes, I get that", said Robert, "But I've got no food in. And I need to buy some..."

"Well, it is for your own safety", said the guard. "We're not doing this for fun, you know".

"Oh right", said Robert. "Safe but starving? Is that it?"

The guard smiled. And shrugged. There really was nothing he could do.

Robert, to his credit, seeing that the situation was completely impossible and, rather than making a fuss, simply turned on his heel and headed for home.

"I can't eat, can't travel, can't work... what on Earth is a person supposed to do?"

Jobless, starving and very tired, Robert finally reached home.

He kicked his shoes off, scowled at the cat, and almost ran up the stairs to his bedroom.

It was true that he had no food in. And it was true that his mobile phone was stuck at the office.

So in some respects he really was stranded.

But he still had his computer, he wasn't desperately short of money, and as for food, well, he could order something online a bit later.

First, however, he would have to fill in his report.

It was unusual for him to be home at this time of day, during the week, and for a moment he sat at his desk and watched the world going about its business in the busy street outside his front door.

Then he pulled the curtains shut and pressed a button on his computer. Which came immediately to life.

A strange, almost triangular face greeted him. A face with great big bulbous eyes and an almost quizzical expression.

"You're early. Is there a problem of some kind?", said the face.

"Oh... it's this lot", said Robert. "They've got a big panic on about a virus and now everyone's wearing masks".

The strange triangular face nodded.

"How can I study humans, if I can't mix with them?" said Robert. "It's ridiculous".

And with that, he carefully peeled off his human face, to reveal his own great big bulbous eyes, set in an almost triangular face...

Lorelei

by Sally Bennett

"Are you ready, Hildy? Your friend'll be here soon."

"Yes, dear, nearly ready!"

Hildy picked up another little white fluffy sock and slid it on over tiny pink toes. She pulled it up and then slipped a finger down the side of the sock to check it wasn't too tight over the sweetly rounded ankle.

"We don't want that digging in, do we, Lolly?"

The baby's round, blue eyes watched her fixedly.

Hildy gently gripped a foot in each hand and waggled them up and down. "We're going out, Lols. To the supermarket, with Anna. And then we'll have a nice little drinkie and a nice little snackie in a nice little café. Won't that be... nice?"

Did the baby burble a happy response?

"Yes. Yes that'll be nicey-nice, won't it, sweetums?" Hildy picked up the baby and smooshed her own face into the firm roundness of her infant. They would have a nice time, doing ordinary things together and even if, just occasionally, Hildy inwardly cringed at the extreme limits motherhood had placed on her vocabulary (she had once been a university lecturer, after all), she was still quite able to laugh at herself. "Nicey, nicey, nice," she repeated, picking up Lolly and bouncing her up and down on her shoulder.

Mark stuck his head around the door. "You taking the stroller, Hildy?"

"No, Anna's going to drive us. And Lolly-pops is going to ride in the trolley today, aren't you?"

"I'll get the car seat."

"No, don't bother. Anna has a spare." Was that her pulling up outside? No. Just a delivery van. It looked a bit grey out there, though. "Do you think I should put a hat on Lolly? Is it cold out?"

Mark shrugged and made an indeterminate noise.

"I will, I think." Hildy sat on the settee, the baby on her lap and sorted through the jumbled contents of the changing bag. "Where's that hat gone, Lolly-pops? Where's that hat hiding? There it is."

Hildy slid the little crocheted hat on and tied the ribbons. She smoothed it over her baby's head – soft, white, fine crocheting that had been one of the first things she'd made.

The scalloped edging had been a challenge at the time, although she could make that kind of thing easy-as-winking today. But the hat was a little faded, now. So when they got home, she'd hand wash it in the sink with the powder for delicates and rinse it out at least three times so there wouldn't be any residue to upset Lorelei's delicate skin.

Hildy bounced the baby on her knee, glancing occasionally through the floral nets that veiled her view of the street. Still no sign of Anna.

She ran through the contents of the changing bag in her mind: nappies, wipes, mat, spare clothes, snack, water, baby sun cream, rash cream. Was there a sun hat in there? Because if it was a bit grey now it could easily brighten up and the crocheted hat wouldn't shade Lolly's eyes at all. Oh, yes, there was one. A bit crumpled. Never mind.

That was all they needed. Wasn't it? She ran through the list again, aware she was fussing now, just because she had time to fuss. But that was her job, after all. Mothers were *supposed* to fuss, because if they didn't do it, who would? And you couldn't be too careful – Hildy was a staunch supporter of that particular old saying and, indeed, of very many others. She looked before she leapt, made sure to place one careful stitch before nine were needed and, since she had first joined the Girl Guides a long, long time ago, she had always been prepared. A mother had to be prepared for anything, to have everything her child needed and to be ready to protect them from the harshness of the world. She would certainly never let anything bad happen to little Lorelei, her precious little angel.

A car pulled up – Anna's white estate car.

"Here we are, Lols. Here's our ride. Oh." Hildy twitched the net curtain aside. "Oh, that's a shame." There was only one car seat; empty, ready for its occupant. "She hasn't brought Flora again. Why does she never bring little Flora now? You two look so sweet together. We could have got one of those double trolleys and you could have sat side by side." Hildy patted Lorilei's gently curving back.

"Hildy? Do you need any help?" Mark was always there, ready to help; always there when he was needed.

"Could you bring the changing bag for me, please, dear?"

Mark smiled and picked it up and held the doors open for her and then helped her do up the straps of the car seat, which were always so fiddly, especially when you were bent over at that awkward angle.

"Have a lovely time, Hildy. Bye-bye, Lorelei." He waved to the baby.

"You're very lucky to have him, Hildy." Anna was smartly dressed as usual. Hildy didn't know how she did it. Her own clothes seemed drab and ill-fitting by comparison, but Lorelei was well turned out – that was all that mattered.

"Oh, I know that, Anna. What *would* we do without him, Lols?" She clicked her seatbelt into place and caught a glimpse of smooth pink arms out of the corner of her eye. Her neck gave a twinge. Maybe she should have sat next to the baby to keep a closer eye on her.

"She's alright, Hildy. I can see her in my mirror." Anna put the car into gear and pulled smoothly away. "Now – shopping first and then a café. Where would you like to go? There's that new place on the precinct we've not tried."

"Oh, I don't know about that. They might not have high chairs. We'll go to Dionne's, shall we?"

Anna laughed. "Tea and a toasted teacake. You're so predictable, Hildy."

"Dionne's nice. She always lets me have a high chair for Lorelei. Not like that Italian place. They said she didn't need one." The cheek of it. Of course she needed one.

"I'm never going to hear the last of that, am I?" Anna stopped smoothly at the roundabout, scrutinised the empty lanes suspiciously and then pulled out. "And I thought you were cross with Dionne for offering Lorelei a biscuit?"

"No, it was that young girl she's taken on that tried to give her a lollipop. Not a clue, that one. I don't want my baby having those nasty sweet things. A biscuit's different. A plain biscuit. One of those big, round ones."

"Alright, then. Dionne's it is."

They pulled into the supermarket car park. Anna drove past the parent and child spaces.

"Anna, no, look. We could've gone there."

"There're plenty of spaces, Hildy. And there's two of us to manage Lorelei. We don't need a parent space."

"Hmm." Hildy bit her tongue. She wanted to enjoy her day and not get caught up in that thorny issue again. Although some people really took advantage, they really did. Great big, able-bodied hooligan children who were perfectly capable of getting in and out of a car – they didn't need the spaces meant for little ones like Lorelei, that was for sure.

Anna found a space and fiddled with her mirrors so she could reverse in. The usual spark of envy flared. Maybe Hildy would get herself a little car. It had been a while since she'd driven, but she was sure she'd manage. Mark said it wasn't a good idea, that she'd get too distracted by Lorelei, but he was just being over-cautious, surely?

"I would have liked to see little Flora again. How is she?"

Anna held the door while Hildy lifted the baby out of her seat.

"She's doing very well, Hildy."

"Oh. Yes. You told me on the phone didn't you?"

Anna pulled out a trolley from the park and hooked the changing bag over the bit meant for shopping bags. She pulled out the seat and Hildy carefully threaded the baby's legs through the holes. It looked uncomfortable. Maybe she should have padded it with a blanket. Lorelei seemed happy, though.

"Did you say Flora was crawling now?" Hildy laughed and patted her friend's arm. "I'm sorry, Anna. I'm so focused on Lorelei, I don't take anything in!"

"That's alright, Hildy, I know you pretty well by now."

The trolley rattled across the car park. Anna pushed it, but Hildy couldn't help gripping the handle on the turns, just to make sure. She trusted Anna, she really did. But when it came to Lorelei's safety, nothing could be left to chance. And when they entered the cool, air-conditioned interior, she insisted on stopping and sorting out a little cardigan from the changing bag.

"It'll be even chillier further in, by the cold stuff; and I want to get some of that nice cheese that Mark likes to have in a sandwich for his lunch."

"He makes the lunch, doesn't he?"

"Yes, because he knows I'm busy with Lorelei. But I always try to get things in that he likes. Oh, look, pomegranates!"

"Does Mark like pomegranates?"

"I don't know, but I was watching that cookery thing the other day and they had pomegranates and I thought, it's been years since I've had one of those." Hildy picked up a large fruit and turned it over in her hands. It seemed to be free of bruises or dents. "This is a nice one." Lorelei's empty hands looked like they wanted something to hold. "Here you are, sweets, here's a pomegranate. Po-me-gran-ate. What a funny word!" Hildy tucked the large fruit into the baby's arms.

"She might drop it," warned Anna.

"She'll be fine. See. She can hold it."

They carried on. One of the trolley wheels kept sticking, then whirling round crazily. Hildy said they could get a different trolley, but Anna said she'd manage.

Bananas had gone up and cauliflowers were a ridiculous price – they didn't even look very nice – but apples were cheaper than normal, in the way they were when the local ones started to come into season.

They hurried through the chiller section and Mark's cheese was on offer, so Hildy got two blocks, knowing it wouldn't go to waste. A woman dithering between Emmental and Gouda looked at Lorelei; and she smiled, which was nice.

Then they were into what Hildy called the cupboardy shelves – the ones that held tins and packets and jars. She grabbed the handle and brought the trolley to a halt.

"Let go please, Hildy. I want to get some tuna."

"No." Hildy turned her back toward the aisle. "There's that whatshername down there, stacking tinned tomatoes – that Brenda who used to work in the post office."

"So? We can say hello? I didn't know she was working here now."

"No. We can't. She said something very hurtful about Lorelei."

"Oh, Hildy, I'm sure she didn't."

"She did. It was very upsetting." The baby still held her pomegranate – such a good girl.

"She can't have meant anything by it."

"She meant every word. She's a nasty piece of work, that Brenda, and I'm not going anywhere near her." Hildy folded her arms across her chest. She wasn't giving in on this one. No chance.

Anna sagged and waved a hand in defeat. "Fine. You wait here. I'll go get the tuna."

"Push the trolley round the corner. She might see me."

Anna rolled her eyes a bit, but did as her friend asked. "Happy?"

"Yes."

Hildy waited. She played a game with Lorelei, taking the pomegranate and hiding it behind her back and then bringing it out suddenly. "Where's it gone? Where's it gone, Lolly? There it is!"

A man with just a packet of Rich Tea and a bottle of whiskey in his basket gave her a funny look, but what did *he* know with a diet like that?

Anna was taking ages. She could have a quick peek round the corner, but that would risk being spotted by that awful Brenda woman. Instead, Hildy sang a few rounds of 'Row, row, row your boat,' to Lorelei. The other verses were a new thing since Hildy had been a girl. She wasn't sure if she entirely approved about the crocodiles and screaming and so on – it seemed like a bit too much excitement for young children, and surely encouraging them to scream couldn't be good? She did it anyway, though, because she was sure Lorelei liked it.

Anna returned with two tins of tuna and one of salmon.

"You could have been to sea and caught them in that time."

"Well, I said hello to Brenda."

"Oh, you didn't!"

"I was only being polite."

Hildy gave Lorelei the pomegranate to hold again.

Anna took charge of the trolley. "She said her youngest's gone into the army."

"Oh." Hildy sniffed. "Well, he probably needs a bit of discipline."

"He was a nice boy."

"Rowdy."

Anna shook her head, and pushed the trolley onward, toward the tempting scents from the bakery. The trolley's wonky wheel jammed and Lorelei jerked in her seat, but kept hold of the pomegranate.

"Stupid thing." Anna kicked the wheel and it freed itself.

Hildy considered the cakes, then opted for a packet of scones, which she should really make herself, but who had time for that kind of thing, with a young baby to look after? Anna chose a French stick, which she was welcome to – such hard crusts, that always made Hildy's teeth ache. Lorelei might need something to chew on, though. Hildy had thought she might be teething the other day.

"Do you think they sell stair gates here?"

"Hildy, you live in a bungalow."

"Well, yes, but when Lorelei starts crawling she'll be everywhere and she might crawl into the kitchen when the oven's on, or out of the front door when I'm not looking."

"I think she might struggle to reach the handle."

"Flora's crawling isn't she?"

"I might get some ice cream."

"Anna, Flora's crawling now isn't she?"

"Some of the really nice vanilla. And some wafers. I haven't had wafers in years."

Hildy put her hand on her friend's. "Anna!"

They stopped in front of the frozen chips. Anna's face had that closed-off look she got sometimes, when her lips went all thin and her brown eyes darted off to look at things which weren't important.

"Anna, is Flora alright?"

"Yes, yes of course Flora's alright, Hildy."

She was looking at the crinkle-cut chips, which Hildy didn't like because she was certain the crinkles made them even more fatty.

"You never bring her any more. You don't even seem to like talking about her."

Her friend's face softened, her brows squashing together like the crinkles on the chips, her mouth drooping at the corners. "Hildy, I do. I do talk about her. I told you all about her when I phoned you yesterday. Remember?"

She'd been giving Lorelei a bath in the kitchen sink at the time. "I'm sorry. I suppose I wasn't listening."

Anna's hand patted hers. "That's alright. That's alright, Hildy. I'll tell you again when we get to Dionne's.

"Yes. Yes, you can tell me again. Are you getting ice cream, then?"

"No. It would only melt."

They found a quiet checkout and paid and left.

The car park was busier and some youths were rolling up and down on noisy skateboards.

"Oh, it's bright. Stop a minute, I want to get Lolly's sunhat out."

"We'll be in the car in a second, Hildy."

"I'd rather get it now."

The trolley jolted again, the wonky wheel binding fast, and the changing bag jerked away from Hildy's fingers.

"Drat this thing!" Anna tugged and pushed at the trolley handle. "I can't get it shifted at all now!"

A skateboard smacked against the kerb, a rude, gunshot sound; the youths cheered. Why couldn't they go to the park? The noise would surely upset Lorelei.

"We'll have to unload here and just leave it," said Anna.

The grinding roll of laden skateboards grew to a roar. Someone should tell them to go. And where were the trolley attendants when you needed them?

A tall shape whipped past Hildy and then another and then there was a yell and a smash. Anna cried out. The trolley lurched and tipped and Hildy snatched at the handle. Her grasping fingers were too late. It crashed to the ground.

Someone screamed.

All around Hildy shoppers stopped and stared. The boys on their skateboards all stopped. One of them lay on the ground, next to the trolley, the wheels on his upside down board still spinning furiously.

"Oh, a baby! There's a baby, look!"

"I'll call an ambulance."

"Someone help! Someone pick her up!"

"Mummy, there's blood. I don't like it, Mummy."

Blood on the ground. Blood on the baby's face, on her head. Her eyes open wide, her skin so pale, her little fingers still; Lorelei, her baby that she'd loved, her little, little baby – so innocent, so precious, so very, very much loved with all her heart.

"Anna."

"It's alright, Hildy. She'll be alright."

"Anna, it was my fault."

"No, Hildy, dear, no, it wasn't your fault."

"Yes, it was. It was. It was my fault. All my fault."

"Hildy, dear, it was a long time ago...".

A laugh cracked harshly into the silence.

"It's just a doll!"

"What?"

"Look! It's not a baby, it's a doll! Stupid old woman playing with a doll! Come on, let's go."

The other skateboards ground away across the car park. Shoppers moved away.

"Silly old biddy."

"Nearly gave me a heart attack."

"Upsetting my little girl!"

"Should be in a home."

The doll lay on the ground, the smashed pomegranate next to her, its juice splattered all over Lorelei's face; juice that looked just like blood.

"Sorry, Missus." The boy picked himself up, and his skateboard. There was real, actual blood showing through the knee of his torn jeans. "Sorry." He reached down and picked up the red stained doll and offered it to Hildy.

Hildy snatched Lorelei and wrapped her arms tightly around the baby and tucked the small, round head under her chin, just as once, long ago, a real, warm, soft head had tucked itself there and snuggled sweetly into her mother.

"Sorry," the boy repeated. He put down his skateboard and picked up the shopping and put it back in the trolley. The French stick was bent. He walked away, carrying his board.

"At least the wheel's not stuck any more," said Anna.

Hildy closed her eyes.

"Come on, Hildy, let's go."

"She's dead, Anna."

"I know, Hildy. I know."

"I loved her."

"Yes. You did."

An arm slid around Hildy's back, squeezed briefly and then released her.

Hildy looked down at Lorelei. "Oh, look at her face, Anna, look!"

"It'll come off. Here, you've got wipes haven't you? That's what they're for."

Plastic crinkled and then Anna was wiping Lorelei's face with the soft, white cloth. The red smears of pomegranate juice disappeared and the white was stained pink.

"There. There you are – all done."

Lorelei's big, round, blue eyes seemed to regard Hildy thoughtfully.

"She's fine now, isn't she, Hildy? There's your Lorelei, all fine again. Now – shall I take you home?"

"No. No, Mark's looking after one of the other ladies this morning. Mary in number four. I don't want to go home if Mark's not there."

"Someone else will be there, though. There's always someone on hand. You're so lucky you got a place there."

"I know. But I want to go to Dionne's."

"Right you are then. Dionne's it is. Oh, look at that, the wheel's fine now."

The trolley rolled smoothly across the car park. Hildy held Lorelei close to her chest.

"When we get to Dionne's I'll tell you all about Flora again, shall I? She's just had a promotion and her youngest did really well in her exams."

Flora had crawled and walked and grown up and gone to school. From there she had gone to university and then out into the world to start a career and a family of her own. And during all that time, Lorelei had remained a baby.

"We'll have some cake at Dionne's."

"A toasted teacake's enough for me."

Anna laughed. "You never change, Hildy."

No. She would never change.

"Maybe we'll have some jam, though?" suggested Anna. "As a treat?"

"Jam would be nice. And a biscuit for Lorelei. A big round one."

They reached the car. Anna put the shopping in the boot because Hildy had her hands full with the baby.

"I think she's teething, you know," said Hildy. "She'll be crawling soon, won't you Lolly? I'm going to get gates for every door. Because you can't be too careful. Can you Anna?"

"No, Hildy. No, you can't be too careful."

Fog

According to all the experts, Camberfell was one of the prettiest and most unspoiled towns in the whole world.

One researcher, who always wore a white coat and called himself a Travel Scientist, even argued that if God herself had popped down to Earth for a visit and looked around for the most perfect, deliciously idyllic setting for a collection of streets and houses, small shops and local services, she would have surely chosen the Camber valley...

Others, who always believed every word a scientist said, no matter how daft or plainly contradictory they often were, also tended to agree. "Nowhere nicer", they all said. Heads nodding sagely in unison, even though most of them would have struggled to find the place on a map.

Scientists, experts, researchers... but to leave such over-heeded folk aside for a moment, it was indeed true that the little town of Camberfell, at the head of the Camber valley, was as picturesque as a place could possibly be.

The houses – in fact all of the buildings – including the bright, fresh (and properly funded) municipal library, the clean, new (and properly funded) municipal swimming baths and the crisp, pristine town hall, staffed by efficient (and polite) staff were all of the same type: handsome stone constructions, often painted white, pastel pink or lemon yellow, with steeply pitched slate roofs, and decorated everywhere you looked with festoons of colourful flowers. Vines, hanging baskets, window boxes... you name it. There were flowers everywhere.

But the good things didn't stop with the buildings, flowers and gardens.

The roads were also spotless (and any holes were quickly repaired – and properly, rather than patched over in a 'let's-pretend-we're-doing-something-about-it' sort of way). As were pavements, parks and shop fronts.

Litter and littering were both unheard of, too. This, no doubt, was in part due to the proliferation of attractive wrought iron litterbins, one below every lamppost, hung beneath several bunches of those bright and cheerful flowers. But it was also due to a sense of civic pride, a thing much harder to quantify. Where did that civic pride come from? No one could rightly say. Was it important? Clearly it was. How did a town keep it, encourage it, foster it? That was a harder thing to answer. But whatever it did require in order for civic pride to prosper, evidently Camberfell had it in abundance.

Then there were the natural features, things which no doubt helped enormously to make Camberfell such a beautiful and happy place.

There was the valley itself, stretching out below the little town, and south facing. That direction made a lot of difference. Facing south means a place has that bit of extra sunshine which helps lift everyone's moods on even the most difficult of days. It also meant the spring came that tiny bit earlier, the summer stayed a few weeks later and lots of good healthy fruit and vegetables could be produced locally and brought into town to the twice weekly open-air market.

Then there was the lake. A big, wild and wonderful blue lake. Fed from springs and mountain streams, the water was as pure as the driven snow. Clean, fresh and wholesome. In itself, of course, the lake helped Camberfell to look very pretty. But it also had the added advantage, lying in the valley below the town, of reflecting daylight back into the streets and homes of the town. So much crisp, bright light that even the air itself sparkled.

Needless to say, swimming was also permitted, without question, in that big, deep lake. As was catch-and-release fishing and canoeing and sailing. (Though noisy and polluting motor boats were not allowed.)

But the real icing on the cake was not the sunshine, nor the deep and beautiful valley, nor the clean streets, relaxed atmosphere, bright light, flowers, splendid buildings or anything else of that type. The icing on the cake was the

Camber mountain itself. This great jagged peak, instantly recognisable across the world, and very hard to climb, being fifteen thousand feet in height and capped all year with snow, stood as a guardian over the town and the people below. Rains from the grim north failed to get past it. Air pollution too, remained on the other side of the hill. The lower reaches gave the Camberfellians easy access for regular exercise on lush green pastures, whilst the upper reaches provided a significant –yet not overwhelming – source of income for the town via tourists and tourism. The skiing, needless to say, being truly superb.

So yes, all in all, where better to site a town?

Where better to live?

Camberfell was exactly as the expert-scientist-researchers had all said: it was just as if God herself had chosen the site for one of the prettiest and most unspoiled towns in the whole world.

Helen Thomas had lived in Camberfell all her life. Travelling away to the big city, for a handful of years, to study and gain a bit of other-placey experience.

The study had been fun. She had achieved a first class honours degree in Observational Studies.

The other-placey experience? A bit less fun. And so she had moved back to the Camber region pretty quickly, more or less content to never travel again.

"Nowhere is as nice as here", she told her mother and father, both of whom were delighted to see their only child move back so close to home. "Everything is so clean, the people smile, the shop fronts are bright and cheerful, the parks, the pavements... oh, all of it, it's all, all so lovely here".

"Oh, Helen", said her Mom, "You don't know how happy it makes us both to hear those words. When you moved away, out into the big world, we were so worried we'd lose you forever and only get fleeting visits at Christmas or when you needed some money, as so many other children seem to do when they leave home and go to university".

"No, Mom. That's not me. I'll never do that. This is my home and I love it here".

Home. Home. Home. One of the loveliest words in the world.

And, later that day, as Helen walked to her new apartment, after a splendid Sunday lunch with her parents, she reminisced about her time in that distant big city, and compared that place to this little town and she saw, once again, just how much nicer it really was here in Camberfell, above the beautiful valley and the wild lake, and beneath the shelter of the great Camber mountain.

"Hello Helen!" a happy voice suddenly rang out. It was old Mr Drear, the man who kept the greengrocers – always open and very busy, especially on the days when the market was closed – and who always stood at the corner of the street and smiled at everyone and had a cheery thing or two to say. "So you're back with us, then?"

"Hello Mr Drear!" said Helen. "Yes, I'm back. And I'm back to stay!"

"Ah, how lovely", said Mr Drear. "And how good it is to see you here again!"

The man smiled and waved.

Helen waved back and continued on her way.

Helen had taken on a small apartment, right on the main square in the centre of town. Ironically, she had lived in an (even smaller) apartment, right on the main square in the big city too. And the difference between the two places was enormous. In the big city she had found herself forever concerned about locking the front door to make sure no one came into her apartment and stole her stuff, or closing the windows even on a pleasant day to shut out the noise and the smell of traffic from the square below. Here, back in Camberfell, she had none of those concerns. The square was quiet and clean. The only burglary in recent years had taken place when a passing burglar had found himself, by accident, stranded for one night in Camberfell after missing his train connection. So Helen slept with her window open, and she hardly ever bothered to lock things away. The front door had neither chain nor spyhole nor triple lock. Nor was it wired up directly to the mains electricity, nor was the handle coated in deadly contact poison. In short, there were none of the usual but occasionally lethal wrinkles or ruses to keep unwanted people away.

And so as she fell asleep that night, she could see the stars twinkling overhead in a deep blue sky and a yellow crescent moon dipping slowly over the valley, almost as if it was going in search of a drink from the crystal clear waters of Lake Camber.

Yes. This was truly home.

The morning, however, told a very different story.

Instead of the almost ubiquitous sunshine, the new day was grey and rather gloomy. Which was very unusual. And, at first, as Helen awoke, she had the horrid sensation of being back in the big city on the dirty old square.

"Oh, thanks goodness for that", she said, as she stood in the open windows and breathed in the silence of Camberfell's quiet streets. "I'm still here. My little town. It's just a very thick fog. It must have descended from the mountain overnight. I shall make myself some breakfast, and by the time I've finished, I'm certain it will be lovely and sunny again".

So she went and had a shower, then she made herself a little breakfast, some muesli and freshly squeezed orange juice, which she ate whilst checking her phone for messages and so on, and then she returned to the window to see if the fog had lifted.

And it had. Of course it had.

The sun was back. The sky was clear once more.

"How lovely", said Helen. "Now, what shall I do with myself.. wait.. what's that over there? Someone has painted something on the road. It's.. oh.. it's just a zebra crossing. Of course it is. I've never seen one of those here before though. Well now, then. What shall I do with myself today?"

Camberfell's first ever zebra crossing had arrived, apparently during the night or the early hours of the morning, whilst the fog lay over the sleepy little town. It had arrived to absolutely no fanfare and people, naturally enough, immediately started to use it without giving the thing so much as a second thought.

It was just a zebra crossing, after all.

Helen yawned, stretched and then decided that she would buy a big bunch of flowers, and take them to her mother to say thank you for the lovely lunch yesterday.

On the way to her parents' home, she noticed there were now zebra crossings in several different places.

"How odd", she thought. The only person to think it.

And it was a little odd, too.

Not particularly disconcerting, but yes, a little odd all the same.

A week or so passed and life in Camberfell went on much as before. Until, one morning, getting up nice and early to start a new job, Helen awoke to yet another fog. Exactly like the last one. Just as dark, just as grey, and presumably another one that had also come down from the mountain.

"Oh dear", she said. "I don't like these fogs. They don't seem quite natural somehow. And we've never had them before".

But soon enough the thing lifted again. And the skies cleared and the sun shone, and everyone had a happy smile on their faces and everything was as before.

Only, actually... something *had* changed.

And Helen noticed it as soon as she left her apartment.

All the zebra crossings now had some sort of electronic control system appended to them. If you pushed the button, a bright red figure of a man appeared on a screen, which meant you had to wait to cross the road. And then, when it was all clear – and most of the roads in Camberfell were all clear, pretty much most of the time – the man changed to green. Then you could cross.

More than that, there were also signs up on some of the roads, red circles, with numbers in them. Lots of signs.

Helen knew what they were, because she had seen them before when she was living in the big city. They were speed limits. Limits which meant that, from now on, the traffic in Camberfell, which did, actually, appear to be a little more frequent than before, would be required to obey not only the speed limits, but also the green and red lights on the zebra crossings too.

But Helen thought no more about any of that and continued on her way to work.

On the way, she passed old Mr Drear, standing as usual outside his shop.

"Morning Mr Drear", cried Helen.

The old fellow looked at her, frowned a moment, and then smiled. "Oh, it's you, Helen. Yes. Good morning". Then he turned and went back into his shop. No friendly wave today.

Helen had only begun her new job the day before. But today, as she went into work, in the bright, cheery town hall, she noticed that something had changed there too. Because now, at the front door, there was not only a man in uniform, who had always been there to greet customers, but there was also a reception desk and a sign. And the sign said, quite clearly and in big bold letters, that visitors must first stop at reception and wait there until called deeper into the heart of the building.

"Oh", said Helen, as she passed the reception desk. "How sad. I always liked the fact that people could walk straight in and talk to whoever they needed in here. It always felt so friendly".

"Yes", said the man in uniform. "I liked it that way too. But things change, I guess. And we must all change with them".

Needless to say, over the next few weeks and months, more of the same sort of thing happened. Life would go along without any obvious major problem of any kind, no changes, nothing, then a fog would come down, and the following morning something else in the town would have been altered.

One day the zebra crossings had iron railings leading to them. So that people were more or less herded to the buttons and the green or red men.

On another day the streets had many more signs on them. Quite a lot more.

And the once spotless road surfaces were now, frequently, painted with speed limits or other symbols of one kind and another.

Access for the general public to the town hall had also been reduced to only a few hours each week.

And the library had stopped opening in the evenings.

Then the swimming pool did the same. And then, at the pool, they even erected signs saying things like 'No diving', 'No kissing', and so forth. Where before, people had only rarely done such things anyway, now they were told not to do them at all.

"What is happening to my little town?" said Helen one day, as she walked home from work, feeling a little sad and puzzled by it all. "All these signs and things. And I am sure there are very many less flowers now in our streets than there used to be...".

"Alright?" A voice cut into her thoughts. A rather curt and almost gruff voice.

It was old Mr Drear. Sitting on a chair, in the open front of his shop. No longer standing on the corner, welcoming and friendly, but quite definitely perched inside his shop like a spider sitting in a big web.

"Oh, hello Mr Drear", said Helen, a little taken aback by the change in the man's tone. "Yes, thank you. I am very well. And you?"

"Hmm", was his monosyllabic reply. "I've been better".

And with that, the old chap got up and disappeared into his shop.

On the following morning, the fog was there yet again. And it seemed, to Helen, to be becoming more and more frequent.

"Oh no", said Helen, as she saw its sinister grey billows from her window. "I don't like this fog. Somehow, every time it comes down and then lifts, my lovely little town has changed, subtly, for the worse. What will it be this time?"

The fog lifted. And Helen set off for work. Constantly looking out for any new signs, or changes, or other rather ill-tempered alterations to the lovely little town.

And she saw lots of things.

Sad things.

First there was the traffic. It was now not all that dissimilar to what it had been back in the big city. People had evidently stopped walking and jogging, cycling and so forth. And now, instead, they took their cars wherever they went.

And as a result of that, Helen had to wait at several crossings for quite a long time whilst the man changed to green. And, as she stood there, she heard people – more than once – fellow Camberfellians, grumbling and complaining.

"No more swimming in the lake, did you see", said one of them. "Not safe, the signs say. Get fined if you do".

"Good", moaned another. "It was a waste of tax payers' money anyway, maintaining the beaches and so on. I never used them anyway".

Then another two voices. Very similar in tone.

"I'm not planting any more flowers this year", said a woman. "I can't see the point".

"Me neither", said a man. "They cost money and I don't see why I should spend my hard earned money just for other people's benefit".

Helen was appalled to hear these things. Never, not ever, not once in all her days had she heard people say such miserable and depressing things. Not here in Camberfell, anyway.

All the same, she tried to ignore the gloomy words and carried on her way to work.

Then she stopped.

Abruptly.

Where Mr Drear had formerly stood on the street corner, there was now a CCTV camera on a pole. Scanning and checking the streets for... for what exactly? Helen had no idea. But these too, she had seen before in the big city. And she didn't like them.

Surely it was more important to trust *most* people, rather than worry about the misbehaviour of a *few*?

And as for Mr Drear? There was no sign of him. He wasn't even sitting inside his shop doorway. Even worse, the shop was now closed and shuttered with a horrid grey steel shutter. And that shutter had been sprayed with graffiti.

"Oh my goodness", said Helen. "What is happening here?"

The sight of the camera and the steel shutter quite changed Helen's mind about continuing to her workplace. In any case, the last few days in the town hall had been quite unpleasant. Plastic screens were now in place between visitors and staff and, without any doubt whatsoever, they had created a much more hostile atmosphere.

On top of that, staff were now required to check in and check out, with every working minute regulated. And breaks, which had once been more or less taken on trust, were now deducted from pay. And there were many other silly, unnecessary, distrustful measures.

"I'm not going in to work today", said Helen. "I'm going straight to my parents' house. I need to talk to someone about all of this".

And so that was what she did. Stepping over more than one, more than ten, more than thirty pieces of litter en route. Something wholly new to the little town.

"Mom! Dad! It's me, Helen", she called as she entered the home where she had grown up and always been so happy.

"Hello dear", said her Mom. "Your Dad is just out, trying to get a problem sorted with our pensions. They seem to have cut them almost in half".

That news was a shock too. Because in Camberfell it was the local council who paid the pensions. And the local council were based, naturally enough, in the Town Hall where Helen worked. And as recently as the day before, Helen had overheard talk that the senior managers were awarding themselves a nice, fat and very substantial pay rise.

"Oh dear", said Helen. "What is going on in this little town? It has changed so much in recent months".

Her Mom frowned. "Oh, do you really think so, dear?" she said. "We've not noticed anything".

"Oh yes, Mom", said Helen, now feeling very sad. And then she told her mother about the zebra crossings, the steel barriers, how Mr Drear had changed, how everyone seemed to have changed. About the swimming baths, the library, the steel shutters and the graffiti.

Her mother sat and listened to all of it without any reply. Expressionless. More or less.

"And then there's that strange fog, Mom", said Helen.

"Strange fog?" said her mother. "What strange fog?"

"Oh Mom, you must have seen it".

Her mother simply shook her head.

"I feel it's like, every time the fog comes down then lifts again, something else unpleasant has been imposed on us all. And it has all completely changed the character of the town... the people. Everything. Slowly, subtly. But in very unpleasant ways. You must have noticed it?"

"Oh, that's nonsense", said her mother in a more-than-slightly patronising tone. "We've seen no fog. Perhaps there have been one or two little changes, just to make people feel a bit safer. To save a bit of money on the rates here and there. But that's all..."

Suddenly the front door slammed. (A thing that had never happened before in that house).

And Helen's father came in.

"Bloody swine", he swore. (He never swore.) "Them buggers. The town hall. The swine. They wouldn't even see me. I have to phone in now and make an appointment before they'll even see a person".

He looked at Helen, but didn't really seem to see her. His expression was distant, foggy, glazed.

"I'm off to the pub", he said. (He never drank.)

And with that he was gone again. Out of the house.

"Mom", said Helen, shocked by her father's startlingly out of character behaviour. "What has happened to Dad? To all of us?"

"Well, really. *We* haven't changed", said her mother in a rather cold tone. "Perhaps it is you. Perhaps you have outgrown this town. Going away to university must have given you ideas above your station, my girl".

Station. That single word.

Helen heard it and, inside her head, the word sounded like a bell. An alarm. And suddenly, immediately, she knew what she must do.

Just two weeks later, having given notice and said her goodbyes to her parents, Helen took a train to somewhere else.

Where? It didn't matter.

What she would find there? She had no idea.

But she knew she would keep moving and keep looking until she found somewhere that didn't have all of those horrible things. A place where people still smiled at one another, where there were no silly signs, a place where people were helped by authority rather than harangued by it, where trust came first. All of that.

And, most of all, a place where people noticed what was going on around them. And stood up against it.

Surely there had to be somewhere like that.

Surely...?

Space race

It really was a special year.

After amassing vast fortunes over most of the last five decades, capably assisted by a range of governments of all different political persuasions, a dozen or incredibly rich men – and they were, mostly, men – had finally decided what to do with their hoards of loot. And what loot it was! Just to put it into context, these dozen or so men had as much money as the other 8 billion humans all put together. On the surface that may have appeared somewhat unjust. Which, to be fair, it was. But that is for another story and another author, because this particular tale focuses on what happened, or rather what *began* to happen in this singularly important special year.

Anyway... the first signs that something supra-ordinary was in the offing were two separate but ultimately intricately linked newspaper stories.

One of these, which almost went unremarked, merely reported that Leo Mink – one of the aforementioned super-duper rich – had decided he would spend some of his spare money on building a base for humans on the planet Mars. Was that a mad idea? Yes, of course it was. But mad ideas are what such an excess of money does for people. It drives them to come up with the battiest of schemes rather than address the real issues down here on planet Earth.

The other newspaper headline? Well, that got a good deal more coverage. (Though not all of it was flattering.) One of those other silly-rich men had been spending a fair bit of time in what he called his garage. This garage was, in fact, a massive underground concrete silo, very much resembling a James Bond set, on a tropical island somewhere or other, far, far away from the source of his wealth. And, finally, in this special year, he had finished his work.

What had he been building? A space rocket, of course. What else?

Admittedly this had been done, very much better, and to much greater fanfare, some fifty years previously, by both Russia and the USA, and done back then – at least ostensibly – in the name of humanity. But that had been back in the day where governments invested money in society, rather than just taking it away from people and giving it, in ever increasing amounts, to these super rich, their businesses and their friends. In recent years, there had been little sign of any government, anywhere, seriously planning to revert to those more caring times, and so the super-rich had decided that they had the whole of space to themselves. Which they did, really. In much the same way they had taken over the once free internet, all the best houses by the sea, most of the land, all the media, sports clubs, chains of hotels and restaurants and so on, they now decided to take over space as well.

Anyway...

In the case of this particular billionaire, Dick Bunsen, his original idea had only been to blast himself up into space – inner space rather than the moon or anything dangerous like that – in order to get a proper view of the vast pile of money he owned. Indeed, it was only whilst sitting up there, looking down on the rest of the human race (literally as well as metaphorically for a change), that he also decided it might be a grand idea to start up a fleet of these inner-space vehicles for very rich people to use so they could importantly get from meeting to meeting around the globe much faster than the rest of us. Though still not as fast, obviously, as things like Skype or Zoom, which could take their face and voice around the globe in nanoseconds. But Skype and Zoom didn't allow viruses to be easily spread, and – as everyone could use them – they just didn't feel *important* enough. By contrast, as only a few of these good folk could afford to travel by rocket that gave the whole silly idea tremendous snob value, and so the idea appealed to them very much.

So Dick went into space.

And meanwhile, back on Earth, Leo plotted his new Martian housing development.

Probably, if things had stayed at that point, Leo Mink would one day have disappeared and pretended to everyone that he was living on Mars and having a great time whilst actually secluding himself on the top floor of a hotel in Las Vegas, as overly rich people are wont to do. And Dick Bunsen would almost certainly have been mistaken, on one dark night, for a bright meteor as his spaceship failed hopelessly and returned to Earth without so much as a splash.

But things did not stay at that point.

Oh no.

Because another, a third, incredibly rich man also launched himself into space for a good chuckle. And soon, very soon, far too soon, a week could scarcely go by without yet another billionaire blasting off. And space quickly became rather busy and that took some of the fun out of the trip for those concerned.

Something had to be done about it.

But what?

That was the point at which Dick and Leo and the other incredibly rich men had a collective brainwave.

The world was full of poor people. Very many of them had no homes, no jobs, barely any food. In fact, they had all sorts of problems. And those problems reflected very badly on the elite group of billionaires. After all, the rich had enough money to put things right. Them and their friends.

But that would have required doing serious stuff about serious issues. Things like buying the entire Amazon rain forest so it was no longer cut and burned for short-term gain. Things like investing massively in great banks of solar panels in the deserts of the world, and paying the people who lived there proper wages to run and maintain the things. All that kind of stuff. Serious stuff.

By contrast, building your own rocket, or planning a hotel on Mars, was much more fun. A real wheeze.

Ah! But of course! Yes! There was the answer!

It was right there, staring them in the face!

So the plan was born. And things were put into motion.

And a mere fifteen years later, everything had been arranged.

No hotel had ever been built on Mars. No rockets travelled to business meetings from New York to Tokyo in under ten minutes. Those original ideas had all been long forgotten.

Instead, those generous and kind-hearted philanthropists had built a whole fleet of rockets. Not little ones, but great big ones which would fly to Mars. And on that planet, they had built city after city. Not just a paltry hotel or two.

And so it was that the last of the world's poor were shipped to Mars on 12 December 2036.

Up there, out there, the poor would still have no food, no work, or other important things like that. But at least on Mars they could be forgotten about. Out of sight, out of mind. Forgotten about while the rich, left behind on a much emptier Earth, played and played and played...

Our end

"So what was it then?" said Jacka, sitting and clicking and clacking as he did so. "I mean, what did you put?"

Alsiss smiled. "Oh, it was easy! And I've got to say, I'm quietly confident."

"Go on then", said Jacka, taking a sip of water. "Tell me."

Alsiss shrugged. "OK. Well... it was the fires, wasn't it? In short, I mean, it was the fires."

Several faces watched her, waiting for more words.

Alsiss duly obliged. "Well... the bit called California was on fire. Again. And that kept on happening, apparently. But by then it had spread up into Canada too. And, erm... Australia, that big island. And... er... oh, of course, the forest in Brazil and all that. The Amazon forest. They were all on fire."

"Lots of places were", said one of the others. "Didn't it happen all over the Europe continent too?"

Alsiss nodded her head in agreement. "Yes. Yes, it did actually. Yes, lots of places."

Jacka nodded. "Fair enough. But why though? I mean why the fires? What did you say for that?"

Alsiss tilted her head on one side. That wasn't so easy to answer. "Well... I think... on the one hand, in the forest, anyway, it was something to do with taking away all of the trees. There was huge amounts of land clearance going on and no one bothered to stop any of that. They cut the forest down, all the animals ran in front of the awful destruction, then they burned some of the wood... and then with the forest gone, I guess they moved forward and cut down some more. And it sort of all got out of hand. And no one bothered to stop it. Like I said."

Jacka nodded.

"And the others?" asked Corah, who had just joined the little group. "The other fires, I mean?"

"Blimey", said Alsiss. "Hang on a minute! Give me a chance! Well.. them... the other fires, I mean, they were busy creating great dust bowls instead of fields, and diverting water away from its normal courses and then using huge quantities of it, of that water, to produce trillions of tons of fruit and vegetables which were then used, really, well mostly, to make sugar drinks and... I don't know, other stuff like that. Unhealthy stuff, you know."

Was that it?

In part, yes. That was part of it.

"But of course, it was a lot more complicated than that", continued Alsiss, "because... as I said... other places were on fire too, and some of those were nothing at all like California and the big dustbowl. I mean, like Canada. I can't really remember... no... wait... it was the weather up there, wasn't it? That was it. The weather sort of flipped out and it got super-hot in places. Even places up north like Canada. So they all, basically, caught fire or began to catch fire."

It all sounded plausible enough.

"Weird though", said Corah. "I mean, the Amazon, that was as different from California as two things could be. The big colonies like Los Angeles, San Francisco, Sacramento, Oakland, all of those places and so many more, those were huge centres of population, belching out their pollution from cars, and trucks and planes all the time. By contrast, where the Amazon was burning, there were no cities, hardly. None or very few cars, and the only trucks were the huge, heavy things that took the felled trees away."

"Yeah", Alsiss agreed. "But it was all pretty complicated."

"Humph. Bad things often are", said Jacka conclusively.

And he was right.

"I suppose Australia, in some respects, that was very much like California. The crops and the water, I mean. And lots of desert," added Corah, almost as an afterthought. "But then, in other ways, Australia was more like the Amazon, wasn't it? Because there were no really big cities. No great amount of people. Not really... Or was it like that? Any of it? I don't know, it all gets a bit jumbled up."

Anyway.

Yes.

It was agreed.

There were fires all over the place that year.

That much was certain.

But then, and in a very determined fashion, Jacka shook his head. "No. No, no, no. Not for me, no. No. For me, it was that virus. The corvid virus or whatever it was. That was the same year, remember. The same year as your fires. But by then the fires and all that sort of stuff were happening all the time so they were used to them. But the corvid, ah, now that was unique."

"Ah... yes!", said Corah. "Do you know, I'd completely forgotten about all of that. I mean that virus thing."

"Really?" Jacka was surprised.

"Yeah", said Corah. She shrugged. "It's really hard to take it all in, isn't it?"

"Hard to remember it all!" laughed someone else.

Something akin to a smug expression passed, briefly, across Jacka's face. "The virus", he said again. "And not just the bug itself either, but all the unnecessary damage it led to. That was it for me. That was how I see it."

Corah, as she often did, wondered out loud. "When you look at it though, really I mean, it all read very much like a disaster in the making, didn't it? Like that big ship. We studied it, remember? You know, the famous one that sank because it hit an iceberg. That was true. But there was also a lot more to it than that. The ship also sank because it was travelling too fast through an ice field. And it also sank because they'd chosen to ignore repeated warnings of ice...."

"The Titanic", said Jacka.

Corah nodded. "Yes. That was it. What a splendid name. I think if ever I get a pet, I shall call it Titanic."

"Be a great name for a mammal!"

Laughter.

"That ship, the Titanic, also sank because of the hubristic idea, which went down along with it, that the thing was unsinkable. So the lookouts weren't equipped with binoculars."

"And because it shouldn't have veered away from the iceberg but pranged the thing head on", said Jacka firmly.

"Lots of reasons it sank", said another voice.

"Yes", agreed Corah. "But that's exactly my point."

Yes. There were lots of reasons the Titanic sank. And it was hard to say which was the *real* reason. Probably all of them were real reasons.

And that year, 2021, had a hell of a lot of the sinking ship feeling about it.

The fires and the virus to name only two.

"I've seen a photo of an iceberg", said Alsiss quietly. "Just a great big lump of frozen water, that's all they are."

Sudden chattering and bustling announced the arrival of someone else.

"Ah! Wait! Hold up! Here's Herry. If anyone knows, it'll be her. Let's ask her!"

"Hello everyone", said Herry, giving a small shy wave as she sat tidily down.

"Hello!" said Alsiss.

"Hiya", said Corah.

"Hello Herry", said Jacka. "Do any good?"

Herry nodded. Trying and failing to supress a big broad smile.

"Knew *you* would", said Jacka.

Herry shrugged and couldn't help but release that same big smile.

No one spoke for a moment or two. But Jacka couldn't let it stay like that, because he was dying to know.

"We've just been talking about it", said Jacka. "And Alsiss said it was all about the fires..."

"Climate change", tutted Alsiss. "That was what I meant by it being all about the fires. The fires themselves were just a part of that. It was climate change."

"Alright", said Jacka. "Climate change then, whatever." He turned back to Herry. "And I said no, the virus. It was all because of the virus and the aftereffects of it."

Herry nodded. "Yeah", she agreed slowly. "Yeah. I can see that. Both things to be fair. Either." She looked at Corah. "And what about you? What did you say?"

"I haven't had my say yet", Corah replied. "You know what these two are like. Once they get started, it's impossible to get a word in edgeways."

Herry laughed.

"Oh, OK", said Jacka, not at all offended at Corah's words, but pretending to be. "I'll say no more then. Keep my mouth proper closed from here on."

"Oh shush", said Corah. "You've never been able to keep quiet, not ever. Not on anything."

They all chuckled. Because they all knew that to be true.

"Go on then", said Herry. "So what did you say, Corah?"

Corah took a long, slow, deep and steady inhalation of breath. Looking, for all the world, as if she was going to give a speech long enough to fill the rest of the afternoon.

"We've only got 15 minutes, mind", laughed Jacka.

"What did you put?" asked Alsiss.

"Politics", said Corah, finally. "In one word, I put politics."

Someone let out a groan. Politics was a very dull subject.

"In what way *politics*?" Jacka wanted to know. "You can't just say that and nothing more."

"Well...", said Corah. "For a start, by then they had gone back, I mean they had gone right around in a circle, back to the days of blaming one skin tone or one nationality or one religion for everything that was going wrong."

"Exactly as they had done 70 years before, with that big war, you mean", said Herry.

Corah nodded. "Yes. They were doing that same old thing again. Blaming one group or another."

"The 1930s", said Herry.

"Yes", said Corah. "Exactly. By 2021 there were tyrants of the old type. Throwbacks to those years. All over the world again. The tyrants springing up, like mushrooms after rain, little dictators with very big mouths, always finding someone to blame for all the woes of their country. Like you say, it was the fault of their black people, or their travelling people, the different sexes, males, everyone, everything, anything."

Even Jacka nodded agreement at this. It was, clearly, a ridiculous way to go on. And they had done it time and time again throughout their history.

"Nor did it stop there either", continued Corah. "Because then the bigger nations, and their leaders, they did the very same thing. They sent messengers around the world to poison people who disagreed with them, or they invaded neighbours on the thinnest of excuses and claimed great chunks of land as their own. They set themselves up as 'President for life' types. And packed off anyone who disagreed to distant prisons. Or they clamoured, remorselessly, on every media platform, about how an election had been stolen from them, always, always, just always stirring up people who were already unhappy."

"Ahh, yes", said Jacka. "To be fair, yes. I'd forgotten some of that. Wasn't there a president who cajoled the more gullible of his followers into rampaging the state building or their parliament or something? Scandalous behaviour for anyone really, let alone a president."

"Yes", said Corah. "But remember, he didn't get punished. The gullible who followed him got locked up, but not him. And so he simply carried on stirring things."

Alsiss shook his head. "Dear oh dear. And they had words like justice and equality too. I guess they really had no idea what those things meant, though."

"Ah, but wait a minute, though", said Herry. "Just to play devil's advocate for a bit, surely they had done all that sort of nonsense hundreds of times before. Dictators and so on. That didn't stop anything then. So why did it in 2021?"

On that point, to be fair, Corah wasn't quite sure. "I don't really know", she admitted. "I guess it was a cumulative thing, maybe? And probably made much worse by the spread of that awful technology everyone was using...."

"Oh don't!" laughed Jacka, who had just taken another drink of water and only with great difficulty managed to refrain from spitting it all out as he guffawed. "Don't get me going on that stuff!"

"Technology", sniggered someone else.

"Oh no! Those phone things! Remember?"

"Apps!" said another.

It was too late. That single word reduced all of them to tears of laughter.

"Apps!"

Ho ho ho.

Hee hee hee.

"Stoppit! Don't!"

"Apps to tell you how many steps you'd taken!"

Ha ha ha!

"Or to tell you when an egg was cooked!"

Ho ho ho.

"Or so you knew where you were!"

Ha ha ha!

Incredible.

Hopeless.

"Oh it was everything", said Jacka. "Little app alarms to tell you to check that another alarm was switched on!"

"Radios you could talk to! So you didn't have to get up from your chair!"

Guffaws of laughter.

"No! Stoppit! Seriously..."

"Another alarm to tell you when your vehicle was going backwards!"

"Oh my. How ridiculous."

"Just open your eyes and look, always worked for me!"

More laughter.

"Oh I know. I know. Don't. And they called themselves intelligent!"

"Intelligent!"

Ha ha ha.

Ho ho ho.

The laughter started again... and took a fair while to subside.

"So, politics then", said Jacka, at last, as the laughter died down, looking at Corah as he spoke. "According to you".

Corah nodded. "Yes. That was how I saw it. What I put."

Politics. Wildfires caused by climate change. The virus.

What else?

Anything?

"There was something to do with currency, wasn't there?" suggested one of the quieter onlookers.

"Covered that", said Jacka. "That's part of what I said. The after effects of the virus. Trillions in debt that they could have all agreed to write off, but didn't for some reason. And so that led to all kinds of problems, for decades."

"Too little food for too many of them", said another voice.

Jacka nodded. As did Corah.

"Well, yes, but there was still more much empty land than actual land in use. It was more of a problem that only a few people owned it."

"I've never really got what money was", said Alsiss quietly. "It seems like it wasn't a real thing, only an invention, a bit of paper, and yet the lack of it... didn't that mean people died and fought wars and all sorts?"

"All sorts", said Jacka. "But no, I agree, I've never really got why either. Given, like you say, that the thing, money, wasn't real in the first place."

"No. I meant a different kind of money", said the first voice. "There was an electronic money or something like that invented, and then... I don't know... didn't that lead to a lot of problems?"

"No. No, no", said Jacka. "That only led to some of them becoming even richer."

"Yeah, but didn't *that* change the way countries were run? Because those people had more money than most governments so they could do whatever they wanted?"

Jacka shrugged.

"It was the climate anyway", said Alsiss. "I'm sure of it. And I said so."

"Nah...", said another voice.

"It was the virus", said another.

Opinions were becoming muddled.

Questions were not being answered.

And as was always the case at such times, as one, and quite suddenly, all the insects fell quiet.

Whenever a conversation ran into difficulty, a deep sound, inexplicable, coming neither from within nor yet from outside of them, calmed everything down. And all disagreement stopped. Indeed the opposite, a sense of complete accord arose and soothed, settled and reassured.

There was, after all, no need to disagree.

It was enjoyable to do so in short bursts. Entertaining perhaps. But it made no real difference. Only dealing with a problem made any actual difference. One solution, the same solution, applied right across the board. Once agreed upon, acted upon. As one.

And as for the reason?

Just what the cause had been?

"Of course, yes", said each insect with one voice. "The reason the humans failed was because they had no hive mind. They would not all pull together like we, the insects, can. Beginning with that year, their world fell to pieces for a number of reasons and the inevitable chaos that ensued virtually wiped them all out. Whereas we, by contrast, remained.

"As part of their madness, they had almost wiped us out. Us, the insects, who helped their world so much. And once they had reduced themselves to so few, it was easy for us to fight back. We destroyed their electricity, poisoned their medicines, and all the time we grew. As one. Until our time arrived."

And with that, the official answer from the hive mind being given and with calm and understanding once more restored, break time for the insect students was over.

History exams were always difficult.

That much was true.

But to explain, in just one short essay, what exactly it was that killed the humans off, well... it may have been a standard exam question, but for each new generation of pupils, it was always a tough one to answer.

"Well... in any case", said Jacka, as he stood, stretched, yawned. "Whatever the reason, it was a very long time ago, when we were still small. We became bigger and now the world is much better, cleaner and healthier – and it is ours, not theirs."

"Yes", agreed Corah, "You're quite right, yes. Art next up, anyway and I much prefer that. History is dull."

The students collected up their things and began to drift away to the exam room in ones and twos.

"Oh, but wait a minute", said Alsiss, "You never did tell us what you put, Herry. You looked pretty sure of yourself."

"Yes", agreed Jacka. "To quote the question, 'What was it that led to the rapid downfall of human civilisation?' What did you say?"

Herry shrugged. "Well, actually, I just sort of turned the question on its head."

Each insect looked from face to face.

"Yes", said Herry, packing her own small bag as she rose. "Well... I thought about all those fires, the climate change, how they destroyed their own environment, then the endless wars... and all that money and the way they didn't share it out evenly... the chaotic, greedy politics, all kinds of things. You know, the way they basically wiped themselves out. And so I figured that, in all honesty, when you looked at it like that, they never really had a *civilisation* to destroy in the first place. Not really. Not a proper civilisation. So that was kind of what I put."

"Oh no! Look at the time!" exclaimed Corah. "Come on, hurry up, or we'll all be late for the next exam!"

If you've got this far.... thankyou!

Please consider giving the book a review on Amazon. It doesn't have to be a written review,- just take a moment to click 5 stars... or 4 stars... or whatever YOU feel is right!

For more information, more books or to contact the author, or just to say "Hello", please feel free to send an email to
geoff@geoffbunn.com

Or take a look at my other books here...

https://www.amazon.co.uk/-/e/B07MR3V247

What is life REALLY like in Sweden?

A YEAR in KRONOBERG - Two Brits move to Sweden and make a new home there. This is a story about snow, ice cream, more snow, sunshine and grey skies. A story about a gate, helpful neighbours, a drunken moose and an angry squirrel...
Available NOW on Amazon:
https://www.amazon.co.uk/Year-Kronoberg-Its-SWEDEN/dp/1792686234/

Printed in Great Britain
by Amazon